DEATH IN THE RECTORY

FATHER DONALD ANDREW DODMAN

ISBN 978-0-9810750-1-3

ACKNOWLEDGEMENTS

Many thanks to all who spent hours reading through
the manuscript and assisted in making the
continuity and shape of this story more readable:

PAULA BERNARD
DEVAN ALEXANDER BURNETT
SUSAN GIRARD
CINDY HONAIZER
NEIL GRAY

DEDICATION

To my friend and colleague, the Rev. Dr. David Hawkins, who, amongst his many interests, collects, reads and enjoys novels that have a Church or Clergy theme.

PART I

ONE

Rain pelted down upon Father Justin as he scurried to catch a bus home after a long and tedious meeting at St. Nicholas' Church in Westminster. He was exhausted and approaching the point of irritability and now to top it off, aside from having forgotten to carry an umbrella, the squall had filled the streets of central London with torrents of swirling water. He removed his glasses and wiped away the mist and droplets of rain so he could identify the bus shelter. Fortunately, it was the one he needed and he quickly slipped underneath the protection of the canopy. The hour was approaching midnight now and the sky was abnormally black.

In spite of the fact that it was only an eight-minute walk to Sloane Square, he decided to catch a bus as his feet were thoroughly soaked now and he reasoned that the short bus ride would at least get him out of the turbulent weather briefly. Justin stood in the shelter for only a short time before he could see a bus approaching. He strained to distinguish the number and soon realized that it was the one he wanted. He uttered a quiet word of thanks and relief. Scrambling onto the bus, he was happy to be out of the rain for however brief a respite. The driver was going more slowly than usual because of the inclement weather and poor visibility, but in spite of that the bus drew up to Justin's Sloan Square stop in Belgravia just moments after he had taken a seat.

The walk from there was just a matter of a few short steps and he would soon be in the comfort of home. The thought of a hot cup of tea spurred him onward. The rain had not let up at all. As he stepped off the bus he was comforted that he was now almost at the Rectory and perhaps Nigel would still be awake and would like to hear all about the tedious evening meeting. He was often curious about church affairs and loved hearing all the details of the inner workings. Justin's heart was warmed by thoughts of finally being at home and hearing Nigel's calming voice and having someone with whom to share the dull events of the evening. It was always a delight to be able to chat with someone who was not another priest with all the usual clerical baggage and opinions; someone who had no ulterior motives and who was simply interested in, and willing to share another's ideas and concerns.

Nigel was a delightful young man in his early

twenties who was between jobs and was lodging for a time in a guest room in the Rectory. For the three months he had been there he had proven to be a very able cook and had an aptitude for keeping the house tidy—his way of contributing to the life of the parish. Nigel had worked in sales in a clothing shop and was well respected by the owner but because of the downturn in the economy it was necessary to reduce expenses and staff and he had to be let go. There had been talk of his coming back again if things improved but it did not seem to offer much hope. Nigel seemed to be continually seeking out other employment opportunities and poring over the advertisements in the London newspapers but nothing had materialized so far. He chose not to return to his family's town in the north because employment opportunities there would be even fewer and he rather liked living in London and had some close friends in the city.

Justin was fond of Nigel and had known him since he became Pastor of St. John's some ten years ago. They often chatted in the evening over a hot drink delving into parish matters and issues of politics and theology. Justin found their conversations stimulating, yet light and good-hearted. It was very therapeutic for Justin to have someone with whom to share the trials and tribulations of daily life. Nigel, too, found those moments vitally important. He had recently shared with Justin a situation that had been weighing upon his mind. He had been to see his doctor about what he thought was a very minor problem—a slight ache in his chest, perhaps acid reflux or something of that nature—and the doctor had suggested that he have an electro-cardiogram just to be on the safe side. As it happened this test revealed that he had what was considered to be a minor congenital heart defect or murmur—nothing earth-shattering—but none the less, something that he should take into consideration. Nigel had been somewhat worried about it for several weeks and he was comforted to be able to talk about it with his priest and dear friend Justin. They discussed the situation until late one evening and explored issues of health and the related questions of the brevity of life and the deeper meanings of existence. It had been reassuring for Nigel to know that he had someone with whom he could share this bothersome issue. Justin was naturally interested and delighted that Nigel would share such a personal thing with him. He felt an immensely strong fatherly response to Nigel and was delighted to be able to be there for him. They came to recognize that Nigel's medical prognosis was probably just one of those things that we all must wrestle with and eventually resolve to live with and accept.

As Justin approached the house he thought it peculiar that it was in total darkness and assumed that he might have missed the opportunity of talking with Nigel. He entered and flipped the light switch in the foyer but to no avail. There appeared to be no power, although he had noticed that other nearby residences seemed to be lit as usual, so it did not seem to be a power outage in the neighbourhood. He fumbled his way through the pitch-black corridor toward the back entrance where the kitchen was to get to the utility cupboard where there were tools and especially a torch so he could begin to unravel the power problem.

He soon found the torch in the utility drawer and proceeded to see if he could locate the problem. A check of the trippers in the electrical box revealed that all the circuits were in the *off* position. He flipped several of them *on* but they immediately snapped back again. Going to the first floor he thought he should check to see if Nigel knew what had happened and to check that he was all right. Nigel did not respond to the rap on his door and Justin discovered that the door was unlocked and Nigel was not there. He noticed that the door to Nigel's bathroom across the hall was closed. A rap on that door got no response either. Justin tried the door handle and found that it was not locked. He cautiously opened the door. Shining the torch around, he was horrified to find Nigel in the bathtub, naked and face down in the water. Dangling by its cord, which was still plugged in, was Nigel's hairdryer—probably the cause of the power outage. Justin unplugged the hair dryer and rushed immediately downstairs to try the electrical trippers again. This time the trippers stayed in the *on* position and lights came back on. He rushed back to the bathroom to see if he could feel a pulse. He did not! He immediately fled downstairs to the telephone to call the police. Within ten minutes two police officers from the Belgravia Station arrived at the Rectory.

"Good evening gentlemen, I'm Father Martin."

"Hello. I'm Constable Morgan and this is Sergeant Smythe."

"Thank you for responding so quickly. I'm afraid we have an extremely serious situation here. I arrived home about a half hour ago to find the house in complete darkness and the power off. But before I go further perhaps you could come upstairs with me."

Justin led the officers up to the first floor to Nigel's room. Peering in they immediately assessed the situation.

"Have you touched anything Father?"

"Only the hairdryer cord. I unplugged it so that I could set the trippers and get the lights back on."

"Good, and you haven't touched anything else?"

"Only the door knob but nothing else in the bathroom—except I did feel Nigel's neck to see if there was a pulse."

"How did you happen to discover this scene?"

Justin reviewed the events of the evening and his trip home after the meeting trying to include everything that might be of importance with regard to his finding Nigel in the bath.

"All right. I'm going to call the Station for assistance because we are certainly going to need more help here."

Justin left the constable for a few moments to give him some privacy for his call and when he had finished he explained to Justin what would be happening.

"Father, I've called headquarters and made arrangements for Inspector Graeme Ingram to join us. He will be here in perhaps twenty minutes. I'm afraid that this might go on for some time, but we must begin to deal with the scene before anything compromises the situation, and of course remove the body."

Justin met the Inspector at the Rectory door when he arrived and ushered him upstairs to where the others were discussing the situation. Justin left them to talk and went to the kitchen for a glass of water. Eventually, the three came downstairs and explained that the body would soon be taken to the mortuary and that things would continue in the morning.

Inspector Ingram said, "Father, considering the hour, once they have taken the body we'll also go but will resume with things in the morning. I presume you will be able to be here then. Do you have morning obligations?"

"Yes, Inspector, I have Mass at seven in the morning, but would certainly be able to be available anytime after eight."

"Good Father. Then we'll be back shortly after eight then. And let me add that we are very sorry about the young man—I'm sure this is extremely upsetting."

"Thank you Inspector. I'll expect you in the morning."

Justin performed his customary pre-retiring routine but on this occasion included taking a sleeping pill as he expected the events of the evening to haunt him. He sat mulling over the events of the day pondering how Nigel could have become distressed so much that he would take his life. At least, it did appear to be suicide. He could not quite imagine what other reason might account for Nigel's death. There did not appear to be any signs of anyone else being in the house—of course, the police investigation was just getting underway and perhaps it might reveal new evidence. The Inspector had ordered the cordoning off of Nigel's room and bathroom as they searched for clues. Thoughts of Nigel and this appalling situation certainly did press upon Justin. He was so fond of Nigel and his cheerful personality.

It was tormenting and troubling to contemplate why he might have taken his own life. Justin searched his mind and rethought recent conversations that might reveal hints of why Nigel might have been driven to do such a thing. His career situation could possibly have been a concern for him even though he never expressed that in any detail to Justin. He knew he had a pleasant place to be for the interim and was surrounded by people who cared for him. He seemed to keep himself busy with his continued search for employment as well as assisting with household chores and especially with his culinary endeavours.

Finally, Justin crawled into his bed and tried to get at least a few hours sleep. Eventually, he drifted off into a somewhat fitful slumber fraught with strange dreams.

TWO

The alarm rang at six leaving Justin feeling as though he had only slept for a very brief time. He performed his rising routine automatically but again, the disturbing events of the previous night dominated his thoughts. By six thirty he had showered, dressed, and said his morning office. He was now ready to go through to the Chapel and prepare for Mass.

Several people were already in the Blessed Sacrament Chapel as Justin quietly entered to remove the altar dust cover and set up the credence table with wine and water cruets. In the sacristy he continued to think about Nigel as he set out a violet chasuble, stole, and began vesting for Mass. Nigel usually served this Mass and also set up for it, but he would have to manage things on his own today. At seven o'clock the Angelus rang out from the tower bell and then Justin made his way to the Chapel. It was December now—just a few weeks before Christmas. It was for Justin one of his favourite seasons. He loved the sense of expectation and the prophetic Advent readings, which proclaim the coming of the Just One who would be the Hope of Israel. In his own personal preparation for Christmas Justin had gone shopping only a few days ago to search for a suitable Christmas present for Nigel. He mused about how suddenly life can radically change.

During the Mass, Justin's mind was only half focussed on what he was doing but all his years of being a priest carried him through. Probably, no one in the small group at early Mass would even realize that anything was out of the ordinary. Justin was slightly on edge because he knew that in a few moments, when he reached the prayers of intercession and prayed for the departed there would be shock waves as Nigel's name was read out. Most of the parishioners at St. John's knew Nigel and few, if any, had anything but complete admiration for the young man.

Mass ended and Justin proceeded along the corridor to the sacristy to divest. He knew that there would be a group of curious and shocked parishioners waiting for him as he emerged from the sacristy.

"Father, what has happened?"

"Unfortunately, as you heard, Nigel has died. It was just last night—and seems to have been some sort of an accident. I'm sorry that I cannot really say any more about it. I'm expecting the police in about 20 minutes and an investigation will begin. I'm so sorry! Please remember Nigel in your prayers.

Justin went through to the adjoining Rectory to make a quick cup of coffee before the Inspector arrived. He settled into his favourite armchair in the sitting room with his cup of coffee on a nearby end table amidst various books he had been reading. He often joked about how he would get several books going all at the same time. He picked up one of them and browsed for a time as he enjoyed the momentary lull—a small distraction from the disturbing events of the day.

It wasn't but five minutes before the doorbell rang and the Inspector and one of the constables who had attended the night before were welcomed and led into the parlour. The Inspector introduced himself and expressed his condolences about the situation. He was a distinguished looking man, probably in his sixties, neatly dressed in a suit and wearing a navy blue overcoat and a hat, which when removed showed a full head of salt and pepper hair which was neatly coiffed. Justin took and hung the overcoat and hat in the entranceway, then escorted the two gentlemen into the sitting room where they could begin discussing the events of last evening.

Justin offered them coffee but they both declined, preferring to get into the business at hand.

The Inspector, without any delay, brought forth a note pad, put on his reading glasses, and began the conversation. "So Father, as you explained to the Constables last evening, you apparently arrived home late after a church meeting of some sort in Westminster. About what time was it when you arrived?"

"I'd say it was about ten minutes to midnight."

"And at what time did you discover the deceased in the bathtub?"

"I'd guess that I found Nigel at about five or ten after midnight. As I explained, the electricity was out and I had to find a torch and then find the electrical box and see if I could reset the trippers. Then I went to Nigel's room, found that he was not there, and then checked the bathroom as the door was closed. I found that it was not locked and so entered. To my horror, I found Nigel submerged in the tub."

"Father, do you have any thoughts about what might have happened?"

"Well, my first thought was that he had committed suicide, quite frankly. And what a place for that to happen! Although, I do realize that there could possibly be other explanations and I'm fully aware that I might also be considered a person of interest."

"Yes, Father, that is a possibility and our usual method of operation is to take into account every possibility.

"Of course, Inspector."

"Now, Father, you were at a late meeting last night. Can you tell us a little more about that?"

"Yes. It was a meeting of about a dozen clergy which took place at St. Nicholas' in Westminster."

"And how long was the meeting?"

"It began at 7 o'clock with a light dinner and did not conclude until about 11:30 pm. Very long and tiresome. I'm not particularly fond of meetings with their endless debate and frequent indecision."

"And so, your presence there could be verified?"

"Certainly. Father Aidan LeBlanc is the chairman of our council, and of course,

the other eleven priests could also confirm my presence. I can give you a list of those who were present at the meeting if you wish."

"Perhaps you could just give me Fr. LeBlanc's contact number or address."

"Certainly, Inspector," replied the priest.

"Now, Father, that will assist in placing your activities at the end of the evening, but can you tell me when you last saw Nigel?"

"Yes, that would have been at about five yesterday evening before I left to have dinner with the Priest's Council members. Nigel wished me a 'pleasant meeting' with a twinkle in his eye and said goodbye. Everything seemed quite normal to me. I mean he did not seem to be acting in any way unusual."

"The autopsy may well reveal the approximate

time of death," Inspector Ingram added.

It seemed somehow peculiar to Justin to be on this side of the questioning process but he realized that this was how things were done and that painstaking methodology was the foundation of police work. It flashed through his mind as well that priests are no different than anyone else even though they sometimes seem to believe that they are above reproach.

Inspector Ingram seemed satisfied with Justin's view of the situation and continued on another tack.

"Father, I'd like to know who else has access to the Rectory—I mean particularly those who have keys, since no break-in seems to have taken place."

"Well, Inspector, there aren't very many. Besides Nigel, and myself there are four others. Chandler Horsham, the church janitor, who comes into the house from time to time to wax floors and clean windows; Mrs. Juliana Bellini, who once a week comes in to look after the laundry; Dr. John Landsworth, a parishioner and lay official of the parish who has oversight of parish buildings; and Bishop Halpin, who was a former Rector of St. John's and who celebrates Mass here on most Fridays.

"Perhaps we could arrange for these people to come here so that we can talk with each of them separately," said the Inspector. "Would you be so kind as to arrange for that? We can decide later on a timetable but it would be best if we could accomplish that fairly quickly and together with the autopsy report perhaps we'll be able to piece together what happened last night, and I'd also like to sit down and talk with you first Father, to explore things at a more convenient time—perhaps tomorrow if that is suitable."

"That will be fine Inspector. I'll contact the others as soon as possible. How long would you want to spend with each of them?"

"I think perhaps half an hour or 40 minutes."

"Depending on their schedules we might have to spread this over two or three days, I'd think."

"That will be fine. I'll be able to fit in with whatever you are able to arrange."

"Oh, Inspector, just a thought—on Friday the Bishop will be here for the 7 o'clock morning Mass. Perhaps you might meet with him over some breakfast here following that. It might be the easiest way of catching him, I'd think."

"Excellent idea. Actually, I'll come and attend his Mass—it has been quite awhile, I'm afraid to say."

"Good, then I can begin arranging meetings with the others immediately and will call you as soon as I have some time slots settled," Justin added.

"Thank you for your assistance Father. I'll excuse myself now as I've some other things to attend to. Perhaps if you are able to arrange any interviews for tomorrow I could come just a little early and talk with you again."

"Certainly, that would be fine."

"Alright then Father, we'll talk to you later in the

day. I can see myself out."

After the Inspector's departure, Justin breathed a sigh of temporary relief. His normal routine, if one can call it that, was eclipsed by this situation. Under different circumstances he had often shared taxing situations with Nigel who was gifted in being a sounding board for Justin. He went into the church and knelt before the Blessed Sacrament for some quiet and much needed solace.

After about fifteen minutes he returned to the Rectory and got on the telephone to begin his calls to arrange for interviews with the Inspector.

Justin reached one of them—Juliana Bellini—almost immediately and was able to schedule her for the Tuesday morning. Mrs. Bellini had also heard of Nigel's death and was as disturbed as the others had been. Calls to Dr. Landsworth might take some time, as he was kept so busy in his surgery.

Although it seemed that virtually everyone knew of the death, Justin had a couple of people ring the doorbell just before lunchtime for handouts and to deliver packages. It seemed odd to him that they had no idea of the horrible tragedy that had taken place in this house. Eventually, he was able to take a moment to have a sandwich. He put the kettle on and began searching through the refrigerator for something to make a small lunch. He found a container with some cold slices of roast beef, which Nigel had meticulously labelled. Quite literally, everywhere Justin looked he saw reminders of Nigel.

He found himself frequently thinking that it was all a bad dream and that Nigel would appear smiling in his cheery way.

In the afternoon Justin continued with telephone calls. Before he began to call anyone he remembered that a parishioner had been admitted to hospital for surgery early the next morning and decided that he would have to make an effort to visit her soon.

Later in the afternoon Justin boarded a bus from Sloane Square to Kensington and to Cromwell Hospital to look in on his parishioner who was to have surgery and also to see another man who had been referred for tests and some treatment for anaemia. It took Justin awhile to find the man's exact location through the rabbit warren of corridors and levels. When he finally arrived at the correct location he found that the bed was empty, but obviously in use, and he was told by one of the sisters that Mr. Gould would be back shortly, that he was in one of the x-ray labs for perhaps fifteen minutes. Some magazines had been left on the bedside table and Justin browsed through one of them briefly until Mr. Gould appeared in a wheelchair assisted by one of the sisters. Once settled back into his bed the curtain was drawn back and Father was able to visit quietly. Before taking his leave Justin offered prayers for Mr. Gould's recovery and wellbeing and anointed him. Justin was pleased that the news about the man's condition was encouraging and that he would be returning home in a few days.

Soon the priest was on his way back to the Rectory for his evening routine of reading his mail and then saying the Evening Office and preparing something for dinner. His evening would again be occupied with telephoning and attending to preparations for his study group, which would meet the following evening.

THREE

Justin woke with a start at the loud buzz and groped about in the darkness for the alarm clock on the night table. Six o'clock seemed to have arrived rather quickly—he felt again as though he had only been asleep for a few minutes. His mass would be at seven o'clock, which left Justin with time to take a leisurely shower and get dressed before walking through the church to the sacristy. As he neared the sacristy he could see a figure in the darkness of the hallway. It was John, the altar server for this morning's mass, who was waiting to get in and set things up. John was about Nigel's age and they had been friends. For a few moments the two of them commiserated about the tragic death and spoke fondly of Nigel. As Justin vested, his thoughts strayed as he thought about how many people Nigel had touched and how much he had endeared himself to them.

After Mass several people lingered to have a

word with Justin and offer condolences. One woman welled up with tears as she spoke of Nigel and expressed her concerns about her own son and his present life situation. Justin listened and did his best to offer support and encouragement to her in spite of the fact that his mind was still preoccupied with his own sense of loss and with the continuing investigation. He was eager to get through to the Inspector to inform him about the partial schedule of interviews, which he had been able to arrange.

There was a little time yet before the Inspector would be in his office, which gave Justin a chance to have a hot drink and a little cereal to fortify him for yet another busy day. As he was finishing up and rinsing the breakfast dishes the telephone rang. It was the Inspector, eager to get on with the investigation.

"Good morning Inspector. I was just about to ring you but you beat me to it."

"No problem, Father. I've been able to clear my day and am anxious to get on with these interviews. I presume you have something planned in that regard."

"Yes, Inspector, I do. I was able to contact all but one of those you wish to see, and I'll surely catch up with him later in the day. However, I've arranged for you to meet with some of them today."

"That is wonderful Father. Perhaps I could talk with you first before the first person arrives."

"That will be fine, Inspector. The first person on

my list is the part-time housekeeper, Juliana Bellini. She is coming by the Rectory at ten this morning so you can come by to talk with me at whatever time is suitable to you."

"Perhaps I could come by at nine then."

"Very good. I can also tell you then about the other interviews I've set up during the course of the day."

"Perfect, Father. Then I'll be there at about nine o'clock. And by the way, Father, I'll be bringing an assistant with me. Bye for now."

"Goodbye, Inspector."

As Justin waited for the Inspector he decided to put the time to use in attending to some correspondence and also to try to contact Dr. Landsworth about and interview with the Inspector. He looked over his file of correspondence; wrote two letters; sealed them in envelopes and addressed them. He presumed that by this time Dr. Landsworth would have arrived at his surgery. Picking up the receiver he dialled the surgery number and reached the receptionist. Dr. Landsworth had just arrived and was hanging up his coat. He soon came to the telephone. Justin explained to him about the interviews that the Inspector wished to conduct with those who had access to the Rectory and was able to set up a time with the Doctor for Thursday morning. They continued to chat a little about the recent situation and eventually concluded the call.

Nine o'clock struck on the grandfather clock in

the vestibule and before a minute elapsed the Inspector and his assistant were promptly at the door. Justin met them and welcomed them. Inspector Ingram introduced Justin to Constable Bell who had come to assist with collecting DNA swabs and attend to other procedural matters.

Justin led them to the sitting room where they could talk. The Inspector suggested that Constable Bell could have a seat in the hallway for a few minutes while he and Justin spoke confidentially and then he could come in and collect Justin's swab.

Taking seats near the fireplace they began and Justin was impressed with the very direct and forthright way in which the Inspector dealt with his questions.

"Now, Father," said the Inspector, "When we spoke last you explained the details of how you had come home late from a meeting and discovered Nigel's body in the bath." In the interim I've contacted Fr. LeBlanc and he confirmed that you were present at the clergy meeting on Sunday evening. I also spoke with another priest who was present and he also had been at the dinner and meeting. So, all is well with that. I'd just like to ask you a few more questions if you don't mind."

"Certainly, Inspector."

"Father, you knew Nigel for some time I gather, as he grew up in this parish. How long have you been at St. John's?"

"Well, Inspector, I've been here for ten years and

have known Nigel since the beginning."

"So you have known Nigel since he was in his early teens then?"

"Yes, that is correct. He was an altar boy and was quite involved in the parish. His parents moved to the north about four years ago and Nigel remained because of his job. He took a flat and lived not far from here, until the job became redundant and he began looking for other employment. In the interim I offered him a room here in the Rectory until he found work and was solvent."

"And how long was he here at the Rectory," said the Inspector.

"Almost five months," Justin replied.

"And, as you said the other evening Father, you had become quite close to Nigel."

"Yes, that is true, Inspector. Living in the same house and taking meals together frequently allowed us to talk often about almost everything. We found that we got on very well together, and I did enjoy his wit and affable company."

"Father, did Nigel have any friends who visited him here?" asked the Inspector.

"Yes, there were a few young fellows he would bring home. There was David and also Todd who I've met, although I'd not have any idea what their last names are or where they could be contacted."

The Inspector jotted things down on a notepad as they cropped up. He finally looked up at Justin with a warm smile said, "Thank you Father for all your help. I'll ask the Constable to come in now and he will take fingerprints and also a DNA swab. The swab is a very simple procedure—just a cotton Q-Tip to collect some saliva from inside the mouth."

"Fine Inspector. I'll call him in, and then in about ten minutes Juliana should arrive for her interview."

Justin interjected, "Oh, by the way Inspector, I almost forgot. I was able to contact Dr. Landsworth and he will be able to meet you here on Thursday morning if that is suitable."

"Oh, wonderful," said the Inspector, "That will fit in very comfortably with my schedule."

Justin opened the door to the sitting room and beckoned Constable Bell to come in as the Inspector went to use the restroom. The Constable explained that although the fingerprinting was a little messy he had hand cleanser to wipe away the ink afterward and told Justin that the DNA swabbing would be simple in comparison. He produced from his brief case the "print" paper and inking pad and soon had Father registered. Then, with a very quick and adept probe with the Q-Tip he had the required saliva and tissue sample and quickly sealed it in a small plastic tube for the laboratory.

Without much delay the doorbell again rang and this time it was Juliana Bellini for her appointment with the Inspector.

"Thank you so much for coming Juliana," Justin said as he answered the door and took Mrs. Bellini's coat. He led her through to the sitting room and introduced her to Inspector Ingram.

"Inspector, this is Juliana Bellini—Juliana, Inspector Ingram. I'll leave you two alone to talk and will be waiting in the kitchen to see you off presently."

Justin ushered them into the sitting room and closed the door. When they had seated themselves Juliana said, "Poor Father, this has been such a difficult time for him I'm sure." Inspector Ingram countered, "Yes, I'm sure it has been. He had known Nigel for quite a long time I gather."

Juliana responded, "Oh yes, Inspector, for quite some years. Well, many of us have. I'm a member of this congregation too and have known Nigel since he was quite little."

"Juliana," said the Inspector, "you probably realize that we need to talk to you as you are one of the few people who have keys to the Rectory. And you must understand that this is simply a routine investigation. It appears that there was no break-in on Sunday afternoon or evening so it is obvious that someone—if there was anyone else involved—could have let himself or herself in."

"Then," Juliana remarked, "you think it was a murder? I had heard that it was suicide!"

"Well, until the investigation is complete we don't really know, but we must keep all options open."

"I understand, Inspector. Oh, it is all so horrible

whatever the details might be."

The Inspector continued, "Juliana, I have a few questions for you if you don't mind."

"Of course, Inspector; whatever I can do to help, I will."

"Thank you."

"First of all, Juliana, I want to ask you how you see the relationship between Nigel and Father Justin."

"Oh my goodness, Inspector, you don't think that..................".

"No, of course not, I'm simply exploring all the possibilities."

"Well, I believe that Fr. Justin was very fond of Nigel. He always spoke very highly of him—and when they were both present they behaved in a very, shall I say, affectionate manner. Oh, I don't mean that....I just meant like a father and son if you will. They were both extremely relaxed whenever I was present. Oh, I certainly don't believe that Father would ever harm Nigel."

"That is fine Juliana," said the Inspector. "Now, do you know of anyone who might possibly have wanted to harm Nigel?"

"No, not at all."

"You understand, Juliana, that I must ask you this next question. Can I ask where you were on Sunday between say 4 o'clock and midnight?"

"Yes, of course, I was with Bruno, my husband all of that time—a quiet Sunday dinner and evening at home."

"Would it be possible for me to speak with Bruno, then?"

"Yes, of course, Inspector. Actually, he is in the car waiting for me just outside."

"So, when we are finished presently, I could take a few minutes and talk with him?"

"Certainly, Inspector."

"Alright," Inspector Ingram continued, "Just one more question before I talk with Bruno. To your knowledge did Nigel ever entertain friends here at the Rectory?"

"I don't really know very much about that as I come in only occasionally to do laundry and things, but I did hear conversations about a few young fellows who were friends of Nigel's, and that sometimes they would drop in to visit. I don't even remember any names.........except perhaps for someone called David."

"That is fine Juliana. You've been a great help."

The Inspector continued, "Just before you go Juliana, my assistant needs to take fingerprints and a DNA swab. It will only take a few minutes of your time and I need to stress that this is routine in an investigation. The Constable will be here in a moment to do that and in the meantime I'll have a word with Bruno. I gather he is parked nearby."

"Yes, Inspector, he is sitting in our green Mini just outside the door of the Rectory."

"Good. If you would be so kind as to just take a

seat here and Constable Bell will be with you momentarily. When he is finished you are free to go."

"Fine, Inspector."

With the sitting room door now ajar, Justin knew that the interview had concluded and he saw the Inspector to the door. They had a word or two at the door and Justin knew that he was off to speak with Bruno for a few minutes and would be back shortly. Justin talked with Juliana for a few minutes until Constable Bell had his equipment set up for the fingerprinting. By the time Juliana had her fingers free of the ink residue the doorbell rang again and Justin let the Inspector back in and Juliana went on her way after saying goodbye to them and wishing the Inspector all the best with the investigation. She also expressed her sadness to Justin and told him to take things in his stride and to take care of himself.

Inspector Ingram explained to Justin that Constable Bell was going to return to the Precinct to do some office work and that he would return in the afternoon so that he could fingerprint and swab Chandler in the early afternoon.

"Inspector," Justin exclaimed, "As we have a little time before your meeting with Chandler, perhaps I could take you to lunch at one of my favourite restaurants."

"That would be pleasant indeed Father."

"The restaurant I have in mind is Thai if that is agreeable to you."

"Certainly, I quite enjoy Thai cuisine."

"It is a place called the Mango Tree in Grosvenor Place and it is just a short walk from here."

"Very good, Father, and perhaps we can chat a little about this situation over the noon hour."

The grey skies had broken up somewhat and patches of blue were beginning to appear. The brief walk to Belgravia would be rather pleasant on this brisk December morning and the obligatory umbrellas could be left behind. Justin was quite eager to talk with Inspector Ingram about how things were progressing even though he realized that as one of the persons-of-interest he should be somewhat prudent about how much he should pry into the case. The Inspector did not introduce the case as they walked through the neat rows of townhouses but preferred to chat about banalities and about the weather. As they walked the Inspector remembered something that he had been meaning to mention to Father Martin.

"Oh, Father, I had a telephone call from Chandler and he asked if I could perhaps come to his residence for this afternoon's interview instead of at the Rectory, and I of course complied. He apparently lives just a short walk from the Rectory."

"Certainly Inspector, that is fine with me" replied the priest.

Inspector Ingram continued, "We'll still be meeting at 2 p.m. so after we eat I'll walk back to the Rectory with you. Actually, I have something to check out there but will tell you more about that over lunch."

"All right, Inspector," he replied, as his thoughts again came back to lunch as they were nearing the Mango Tree.

Justin commented that he was quite partial to Thai cuisine and that he frequented this restaurant fairly often. They were soon at the door and went inside. A cordial young Thai woman welcomed them and offered to help hang up coats. The Inspector noticed, as Justin also had done, that the young lady had a decidedly Yorkshire accent which struck them both as being a curiosity. They were then seated in a pleasant alcove and brought menus. The waitress asked about beverages and the two men declined drinks but asked for some mineral water with ice and lemon slices. They were left to mull over the menu while the water was prepared.

"This looks quite intriguing," the Inspector remarked.

"Yes, it certainly is," Justin offered. "I'm very fond of the Tom Ka Goong soup. It is quite spicy with prawns. And my favourite main dish is Nuer Pad Nam Man Hoi, which is stir fried sirloin beef fillet with ginger."

"There certainly are quite a few choices on this menu," remarked the Inspector. "Oh, here is the water. We might even need another bottle of mineral water to go with all these spicy dishes."

The young waiter who came to take their orders

introduced himself as Thomas and then asked what they would like to start with. The Inspector said that he thought he would have the Som Tum appetizer and then the char-grilled swordfish. He quipped, "I won't attempt to pronounce the Thai name!"

Justin chose his favourite starter, the Tom Ka Goong soup, and the Gae Yang roasted lamb. He asked the waiter if they might have a small order of the peanut sauce and some plum sauce as well. The young man repeated everything and went on his way to the kitchen.

Inspector Ingram sipped at his water and finally opened up a little about the investigation. "Father, I'm not quite sure where everything is going at the moment; however, a few cracks seem to be opening up as we proceed. When I spoke with Juliana I asked if Nigel had any friends who might have occasionally visited at the Rectory. She said that she was aware from conversations that there might be a few. She seemed to recall hearing mention of a David. Does that ring true with you Father?"

"Yes, it does. I've encountered David several times before. He was a pleasant young man about Nigel's age. They seemed to get on well together and had similar interests. They would sometimes go out on a Saturday evening if I recall correctly. Of course, no one was keeping tabs on Nigel so where they went was of no concern to me."

"Do you know where this young man could be

reached Father, or what his surname might be?"

"No I don't know his full name, nor where he lives, Inspector, but come to think of it, I believe Nigel had a mobile. Perhaps David's number would be entered there. Did you come across that phone in your look around Nigel's room?"

"Actually, no. We were really at that point simply looking for anything suspicious that might have been connected to the scene in the bathroom."

"I understand," Justin retorted. "Perhaps when we go back to the Rectory you could look in again and see if the phone is there.

"Good idea, Father. And perhaps if we do find the phone there might well be other contacts that could prove useful."

In several minutes the waiter appeared with steaming bowls of rice and an assortment of sauces and condiments. The various dishes came in quite rapid succession and they tucked in to a pleasant lunch. The Inspector commented favourably about Justin's choice of venue for their lunch and conversation was casual and rather minimal as they dealt with their meal. The sun began to break through the cloud cover and a stream of sunlight probed through an upper window illuminating a corner of their table. Justin thought to himself that it was a good omen in the midst of the unsettling events of this horrible week.

The walk back to the rectory was quite pleasant now that the heavens seem to have parted somewhat. Inspector Ingram commented that London—even in the midst of winter—could be quite pleasant when the sun is shining. Justin quite agreed and expressed his thought that this was like a ray of hope in the midst of such an unhappy time.

There was now almost an hour before the Inspector had to be at Chandler's home for his interview. He thought that this would give him time to look around again in Nigel's room to see if he could find his mobile. Justin unlocked the front door of the Rectory and took the Inspector's hat and coat so that he could then go upstairs to Nigel's room. The phone did not appear to be on the dresser or the bedside table so he began looking into drawers and almost immediately he found the phone under the neatly placed and folded underwear. He went back downstairs where Justin was waiting in the foyer. He was preoccupied at first trying to figure out how to open the memory to see if there were any names listed. As he tried the various commands all of a sudden a number of names appeared.

"Oh, Father, I found the mobile and I've just discovered how to open the memory function," said the Inspector. "I see that your name and number are here amongst several others including that friend David. I'll examine things further later on after I've had a chance to interview Chandler. One of the constables will be meeting me at Chandler's home to look after the fingerprinting and DNA swabbing. So, Father, I'll continue on my way and will be in touch

with you probably tomorrow. By the way, thank you
so much for the delicious lunch. Again, let me say
that your choice was excellent. I can understand
why you frequent the Mango Tree."

Justin saw Inspector Ingram to the door and
bade him farewell as they tentatively decided upon
their next contact. When the Inspector had set off
Justin went to his desk and began to map out the rest
of his afternoon. He was becoming decidedly behind
with a number of things since all of this drama had
begun. Perhaps he would spend most of the
afternoon on the telephone dealing with business
and parishioners who had of necessity been put on
hold for the last few days.

Chandler and his wife Rose lived in a row house
a few minutes walk to the west of the Church and
Rectory. Inspector Ingram continued on his way
quite enjoying the fresh breeze, which undoubtedly
had chased the clouds away and opened up the sky.
He was more than happy to have these few moments
of solitude and exercise—the walking was a rather
pleasant change from his usual routine. It was
broken for only a few moments by a traffic
altercation. It seemed that two drivers had designs
on one of the few parking spots to be found in this
part of Kensington. He wisely ignored it and left the
two men to resolve their dispute about who saw the
spot first and continued on his way. The directions
Chandler had given were very easy to follow and he
soon found himself in front of 33 Cadogan Lane. A

few steps above street level he found the blue door that Chandler had emphasized so carefully and rang the bell. He was quite on schedule and Chandler was quick to answer the bell and welcome Inspector Ingram into a pleasant foyer—the odour of the mid-day meal still perceptible in the air. Mrs. Horsham was a few feet behind Chandler to welcome the special guest.

"Rose, this is Inspector Ingram; Inspector, my wife Rose," Chandler ceremoniously announced as he introduced them.

"So nice to meet you, Mrs. Horsham," responded the detective. "I had a most pleasant walk through your neighbourhood—and the weather has certainly improved in the last few hours."

Chandler led the Inspector through the entranceway to the sitting room followed by his wife. Rose offered refreshments but the Inspector declined, explaining that he had not that long before had lunch. He thanked her though, and she soon made an excuse to leave them alone to talk. Chandler offered a chair for the Inspector and sat nearby himself. Inspector Ingram explained that a forensic constable would be arriving before too long and explained about the routine procedures for fingerprinting and collecting of DNA swabs. Chandler did not appear to have any problem with that. He had undoubtedly become acquainted with such routines from crime shows on television. Once that matter had been settled Inspector Ingram began his questioning. "Chandler, I understand that you have been associated with St. John's for quite some time. Would you kindly tell me a little about that?"

"Certainly Inspector. Well, I was brought up from childhood in this neighbourhood and have been a part of St. John's as long as I can remember. I was an altar boy when I was quite young and the church just seemed to be a second home to me. When I was in my mid 20s I was volunteering with many of the odd jobs around the church, as I was handy with carpentry and such things. Eventually, the Priest at that time, Father Conan, offered me full time work as a caretaker or janitor if you will. I've been at that now for some 25 years. That is why I'm one of the few people who has keys to the buildings."

The Inspector, picking up on that said, "Yes, that is of course why we need to do the fingerprinting and DNA swabs. Of course, as you have access and are often in the Rectory to do cleaning we quite understand that we'll find your fingerprints about, so do not be concerned about that—this is a routine procedure."

"I understand, Inspector," he responded.

"Now Chandler, perhaps you could tell me a little about Nigel, his residing here and perhaps some of your thoughts about what happened," the Inspector enquired.

"Well, Inspector, I don't quite know where to begin. Of course, I've no idea what really happened. I've just heard rumours of various sorts about the bath—some about drowning and others about electrocution."

The Inspector interjected, "Well, Chandler, I didn't mean what you think happened last Sunday evening so much as how you felt about Nigel living in the Rectory."

"Oh, I see Inspector," he added, "Well, it is difficult to say really, except that I do, or I did feel somewhat awkward about the whole situation of Nigel living in the Rectory, especially now that this situation has been reported in the newspaper and I know that gossip is circulating. I did feel resentment about Nigel staying in the rectory and was concerned for Father Justin who I felt was being used. I hate to say it Inspector, but from the beginning...I mean since Nigel came to live in the Rectory I've felt considerably uneasy. I suppose I was protective of Father and concerned about his reputation. As well I wondered how all this might appear to the other people of the parish. I've not actually heard anyone comment about Father and Nigel living together, but I've been quite uneasy about it myself. That was really why I felt that I'd rather talk to you here than at the Rectory. I just feel very uncomfortable about it. I feel bad in bringing these things up you know, because although I'm extremely sorry about what happened to Nigel, it still does not sit well with me. They seemed to be very close and, well, chummy. I knew that Father thinks, or thought, very highly of Nigel.

It's just that—well you know—people are prone to talk. I must admit that in this last while I've often felt awkward when I had to come into the Rectory to wax the floors or do cleaning—I mean, one just doesn't know what one might stumble across." But, I'm very sorry about Nigel's suicide. That is what it was, isn't it Inspector, a suicide?"

The Inspector was quick to add, "Well, I do appreciate your thoughts about the situation Chandler, but you know, the case is far from over. I mean suicide certainly is a possibility, but we really don't know yet. It is a little complicated and certain things are yet to be reckoned with."

Inspector Ingram continued, "What about Nigel's friends? Have you ever seen any of them?"

"Yes" Chandler answered, "At least one of them. I think his name was David. Now, I don't mean to be critical or mean spirited, but David did seem to be a little bit....how shall I put it....effeminate! It really does make me feel a little awkward even though I certainly never had any reason to think that there was anything untoward going on......it is very difficult to say anything helpful, I realize." I certainly am not suggesting in any way that I think Father Justin might have been involved in Nigel's death—to me that idea would be very odd indeed."

"Alright, Chandler, you've been very helpful, thank you," the Inspector said, as he seemed to be concluding the interview. He continued, "I have just one more question that I must ask, and that is where you were on Sunday afternoon and evening."

Chandler replied, "Well, Rose and I were here all day except for going to Mass at St. John's in the morning. Would you like to speak with Rose?"

"I'll have a word with her while you are working with the constable and the fingerprints. I think I heard the doorbell a few minutes ago which was probably the constable."

"I'll check and see if he's here Inspector, and call Rose down if she is upstairs, Chandler offered."

"Thank you Chandler, that has been very helpful," the Inspector said as they stood and moved toward the door.

Rose was in the foyer talking with the constable as Chandler and the Inspector emerged from the sitting room. Once introductions were made all around, the forensic constable suggested that he and Chandler might go to the kitchen to do the sometimes messy fingerprinting and the Inspector and Rose went into the sitting room to chat.

Rose and the Inspector sat on the divan for the brief interview. They began with some small talk about the sad situation and then some questions about how long Rose had known Nigel and her views about what might have happened. She had known both Nigel and Father Justin for many years and was extremely sad about the events of the week. Rose did not really know what to make of it and did not have any theories or opinions as Chandler had although she did give the Inspector the impression that she thought that Nigel had taken his own life. Finally, Inspector Ingram worked his way around to the crucial question for Rose, which was where Chandler had been on Sunday afternoon and evening. She responded that Chandler had been in all day with her except for the morning when they had gone to Mass. Rose seemed a little agitated that the Inspector might think that Chandler had somehow been involved in Nigel's death but was reassured that it was simply a routine matter to ask such questions and to take fingerprints and DNA samples since Chandler was one of the few people known to have keys to the church buildings and Rectory. She seemed to be satisfied with that and soon they could hear Chandler and the Constable talking in the foyer. The Inspector rose and they joined the others. After the usual cordialities they bid each other goodbye. Once they had gone Chandler looked at Rose in bewilderment and said, "Well, it is all a disturbing situation isn't it? I felt rather like a criminal having my fingerprints taken— that's the first time I've ever been asked to do that."

Rose replied, "And I felt a little awkward myself as the Inspector asked me about your whereabouts on Sunday—but I suppose it is all a part of their investigation. It will be a relief to finally know just what did happen on Sunday evening."

✠

Constable Bell had a vehicle and was going back to Headquarters in Westminster so the Inspector took the opportunity to have a ride back to Victoria where he would take the Tube to his home in the suburbs at Hampstead. It was now late in the afternoon and he needed to get home and have a little supper before he attempted to contact some of the people who were listed on Nigel's mobile.

Luckily, there was no waiting after he had descended to the level of the Northern Line and a train came along almost immediately. He managed to squeeze in along with a hoard of rush hour commuters and was thankful that the ride to Hampstead station would not be too long. As the train rumbled along the Inspector thought about what he might pull together for an evening meal once he had relaxed with a scotch. His wife had died a year and a half ago, and he was now getting used to dealing with the groceries, and preparing the sort of meals he enjoyed. He was careful to be disciplined about groceries and the preparation of meals and had managed to have a good routine and eat a balanced diet. It had taken some doing getting used to this after Mary had died, but he found that he took rather some pleasure in it. Friends had even noted on occasion that he was becoming somewhat of a chef. However, this evening would be something simple as he had work to do. He mused about a dinner party he had hosted a few weeks back when three friends came to his house and how he was so pleased with how the chicken dish had turned out. It was a satisfying occasion and he did appreciate the compliments; particularly those from the female guests.

Hampstead Station was the next stop and the Inspector carefully edged his way through the crush toward the doors so as to be able to get out quickly. As he took the stairs up to street level he was reminded that he had intended for the past week to buy some cushioned insoles for his shoes and decided to stop by the Boots shop in the High Street, which was only a short distance out of his way. He found what he needed quite quickly and returned to the street to walk the short distance to his flat in Flask Walk. Although he had done quite well in adjusting to being without Mary it was still an odd feeling to come home to a darkened house. By reflex he was still often prone to announce his arrival as he turned the key and entered the flat. After a brief rummage through the refrigerator he found some things that would make a pleasant dinner with a little microwaving. But, first things first—he poured a little libation to ease him into the dinner hour.

Some leftover chicken and vegetables from the evening before provided a rather pleasant meal accompanied by a slice of hearty bread and butter. He decided to call this 'David' as he seemed to be the person most mentioned by the others he had interviewed so far. It appeared that David was perhaps Nigel's closest friend.

Eventually the clock in the study struck 7:30 p.m. and the Inspector decided to try some calls to see if he could reach any of Nigel's friends. He went to the hallway where he had left his briefcase on a bench and searched around in the dark for Nigel's mobile. Settling himself again in the armchair he toyed a little with the phone and jotted down the numbers for David, Jason and Todd. He dialled David's number first and the phone at the other end rang three or four times before a voice rather hesitantly answered: "Yes!"

"May I speak to David please," asked the Inspector.

"Yes, this is David."

"David," continued the Inspector, "I'm Chief Inspector Ingram of Scotland Yard. Sorry to bother you David, but have you perhaps heard the news about Nigel?"

"Yes, I have Inspector. When I heard the news from another friend of ours I really didn't know what to do. I didn't want to call the Rectory and bother Father Justin, who I imagine is having a terrible time of it himself."

The Inspector quite understood David's reaction, and continued. "David, I'd like to have a chance to talk with you sometime soon as I understand that you knew Nigel quite well."

"Certainly, Inspector, I'd be happy to do that."

Inspector Ingram suggested that perhaps they might be able to meet somewhere convenient the next day in the afternoon or evening. David said that the afternoon would be fine and they decided that David would drop by the Inspector's office at headquarters in Westminster at 2 pm. David jotted down the particulars about the office on the 3rd Floor of the Yard building. Before they terminated the call David asked if he might just ask a brief question to which the Inspector replied in the affirmative.

David said, "I know that news gets passed on rather carelessly sometimes but is it actually certain that Nigel committed suicide?"

The Inspector said, "Well, David, that could be, but the investigation is still underway and we cannot really be certain. It could have been an accident for that matter and, of course, there are even other possibilities but we'll continue to follow all possible leads."

David seemed to be a little relieved to hear even that, and he continued, "Well,

Inspector, I find it rather difficult to believe it could have been suicide. But, I'm sure we'll get into that more tomorrow when we meet. And thank you, Inspector, for calling me. This has constantly been on my mind since I heard the news and I'm glad to hear from someone." I'll see you tomorrow afternoon then!"

"Thank you David, for your cooperation, and

we'll meet tomorrow around 2 in the afternoon. Oh David, before I forget, I don't know what your surname is—you were simply listed on Nigel's mobile phone by first name."

"Oh, of course Inspector—my last name is James —David James."

"Thank you David, then we'll see you tomorrow afternoon, Goodbye David." "Goodbye Inspector.

Graeme was rather glad that he had reached David so easily and he was pleased that he was so concerned. It might be a new window into the case tomorrow when they would be able to delve into the situation more deeply. Perhaps David might even be able to shed some new light on things. He continued making calls to some of the other people listed on the phone but was not successful in reaching anyone. He decided to read until it was bedtime.

FOUR

Justin's day began as usual with a quick shower and his morning office in the Chapel. During his meditation before Mass Justin could not keep his mind from wandering back to thoughts of Nigel and the continuing investigation. He was sorely troubled with it all and it was beginning to show. He hoped that his concern and distress was not visible to his flock, although he was well aware that they empathized and were praying for him as well as for poor Nigel.

It was now time for him to prepare for Mass. He crossed himself and rose to go to the sacristy to lay out vestments and prepare the vessels. On his way he met one of the parishioners in the ambulatory and had a brief chat, which ended with the woman's assurance that he was in her prayers.

After Mass Justin managed to slip away from the gathered worshippers and go back to the Rectory and continue work at his desk. The correspondence was piling up and he had lately fallen far short of his disciplined reading schedule. Upon completing several letters he picked up the current book he was reading—"*Souls of the Damned*"—but soon put it aside because it was not really the sort of thing he needed at the moment. He instead picked up the phone and called his mother to chat and perhaps try to share his loss with her and get some motherly consolation. They chatted at some length and then concluded their call. Justin was calmed considerably as was usual when he talked with his mother.

He had hardly hung up the receiver when the phone rang and it was the Bishop. He had heard the news—as it seemed everyone had—and expressed his shock and sorrow. The Bishop, of course, had known Nigel for years and was fond of the young man's bright personality and charm. Bishop Halpin asked Justin if it might be possible for him to drop into the Chancery Office for a short time that afternoon to talk a little. Justin assured him that he could and they decided upon a time.

The weather, being fair again, made it a pleasure to walk into Westminster to the Chancery Office. He thought to himself that it was almost Spring like. He presented himself at the main desk in the foyer and a secretary called the Bishop to announce Justin's arrival. She sent him on his way and he climbed the stairs to the second floor. The Bishop was at his office door and welcomed Justin warmly. "Do come in Father," said the Bishop shaking Justin's hand and putting his other arm around his shoulders in a fatherly hug. "Have a seat here on the lounge."

"Thank you Bishop." Bishop Halpin continued, "I heard the news about Nigel and wanted to express my sorrow and see how you are handling the situation." He continued, "It is such a shocking turn of events, I'm told that it was possibly a suicide—is that true?"

"Well, Bishop, it does seem that way although the Inspector is very careful to remind people that the investigation is not complete yet and that there may well be other possibilities," replied the Priest.

"If I can be of any assistance, Father, please let me know. I mean apart from keeping you and your people, and of course poor Nigel, in my prayers."

"You are too kind Bishop, and I do appreciate your concern," Justin said. "I've been quite stressed about everything—but then, we are prepared and strengthened in this work for such events. I'm sure I'll weather the storm. It is just a little rough at the moment. But the parish is extremely supportive and I'm thankful for that."

They continued to talk and reminisce for a time and Justin did feel so much better for the Bishop's genuine concern. As he walked back through the townhouses and the neighbourhood sounds on this beautiful, sunny afternoon, he thought to himself that there are times when even Father needs a Father's touch.

Justin arrived back at the Rectory to find that

the post had come and he looked it over as he had a hot drink. He sat in the parlour in his favourite comfy chair and after perusing the mail he had ample time to make some notes and flesh out the material that he would propose for the theological discussion group meeting, which took place once each fortnight on Wednesday evenings. He wanted to be prepared with material for the night's discussion even though he knew that in all likelihood they would not want to discuss anything other than what had happened on Sunday evening. He was certainly not looking forward with any pleasure to this meeting which normally he rather relished as he had an aptitude for teaching. Usually he relished this gathering because he was buoyed up by the interest and eagerness of the small group aside from the fact that he quite enjoyed exchanging ideas and opinions. Justin was convinced that the mood of this evening's meeting would be somewhat painful as it would undoubtedly be an occasion when Nigel would be discussed in depth and all the nightmarish reality of his finding of Nigel's body in the bath would be revived. They would perhaps be gentle about pressing the discussion too far because most of them were aware of Father's fondness for Nigel.

✠

David James was on his way to his interview

with Inspector Ingram. He took a bus into Westminster after his lunch and found that his timing was quite spot on—he arrived at Scotland Yard with about eight minutes to spare. He found his way to the Inspector's office and presented himself to the constable at the main desk. The constable obviously knew of the appointment and checked David's name with the appointment book. He asked David to take a seat and said that he would check with the Inspector and be back in a moment. The constable disappeared down a hallway and was soon out of sight. David had felt a little intimidated coming to Scotland Yard and was curious to notice the ambience of the place. His only impressions about such places was from television and he seemed to be amazed that it was all very much like it is depicted, including the jangling phones and the conversations of the staff in the open office area.

Soon the constable returned and told David that Inspector Ingram would see him and gave him directions to office number 321. He soon found the office and found the door ajar and the Inspector behind his desk waiting. David knocked and said, "Hello, Inspector, I'm David James."

"Good afternoon, David, I'm Inspector Ingram, thank you so much for coming in to talk about this unfortunate incident."

"I'm happy to be of assistance Inspector," he replied.

"Please have a chair David", said the Inspector,

motioning to a particular chair near his desk. Inspector Ingram sat down in his chair at the desk and began the interview without any delay. "As we discussed on the telephone I know that you heard the unhappy news about Nigel. May I ask how you came to know of his death?"

"Certainly, it was a telephone call from a mutual friend of ours, Todd Marshall. I'm not really sure how he came to hear of it," David replied.

The Inspector looked down at his notes spread out before him and said, "Yes....Todd—I found that name also on Nigel's mobile, and will be contacting him as well. I haven't had any luck in reaching him yet."

Inspector Ingram continued, "David, do you have any thoughts about what might have happened on Sunday evening?"

"As I said on the telephone, Inspector, I don't have any reason to believe that Nigel would take his own life. I just can't believe that it was suicide, and I hope that, as you said, there must be another explanation. I mean Nigel was happy with himself. He was of course concerned about the work situation, but he didn't let it get him down. He always believed that he would find employment, and he was quite happy to be able to stay at the Rectory and was quite close to Father Justin."

"I see," interjected the Inspector.

"David, you and Nigel were also quite close, weren't you?

"Yes, we were very good friends and chummed around with Todd and Jason Grant, who I presume you have also found a telephone number for from the mobile."

The Inspector again consulted his notes and said, "Yes, Jason. I have only the first names here, but thank you. So it is Jason Grant. I'll also be trying to contact him.

"David, can you tell me a little about your friendship with Nigel, and for that matter with Todd and Jason?"

"Well, Inspector, Nigel and I, and for that matter, sometimes all four of us would go on a Saturday night to visit some of the clubs in Pimlico and Soho. Often we would go to our favourite bar in Pimlico."

The Inspector hesitated for a few moments as he scratched his chin and then said, "Aren't there quite a number of gay establishments in Pimlico, and in particular the *Clipper*!"

David blushed a little and then added, "Oh, you know about those places then Inspector."

"Yes, all part of my work to know these things. Now, I don't mean to pry David, but in light of all the circumstances I must ask you a few personal questions."

"That is quite alright, Inspector, do go ahead."

"Well," said the Inspector, "Did you and Nigel have a *special* relationship?"

"No, we didn't Inspector, but I'll be quite up front with you. I was very fond of Nigel but the truth of it is that we were really just good friends. Had I had my way it might have been quite different, but you see, Nigel was attracted to older gentlemen. I understood that completely but we were very close."

"What about Nigel's relationship with Father Justin if you don't mind me asking?"

"Well, I must say, Inspector, that I've often wondered about that too. They were very close and happy when together, but Nigel never, ever revealed anything personal between them. That would have been quite off limits. Nigel was very discreet and that sort of prying I simply never would have done. As I said, whenever I saw them together they were always very respectful and I think, truly enjoyed each other's company. Nigel was very happy at the Rectory. Father Justin must be very troubled about things and that's why I never attempted to call him after I heard the news. It is all so sad."

"I know what it must be like for you David, and I'm so very sorry," said the Inspector and then continued, "I do appreciate your candour, David, as well as coming in for this interview. You have been very helpful and I appreciate it. Hopefully we'll get to the root of the situation eventually."

"Thank you Inspector, I've probably not been of much help. I'm still puzzled and dismayed about the whole situation," David said as he moved toward the door. "Good luck with the investigation, and if I can possibly be of more assistance don't hesitate to call me."

Inspector Ingram walked with David to the front desk area and again thanked him as he bade him farewell. He went back to his office to ponder and digest this new information. Again, he scrutinized the many jottings and details he had been gathering trying to possibly see them anew in the light of information that David had been able to offer. What if Father Justin thought that Nigel was having a relationship with David and was so smitten with Nigel that he was envious and jealous, that he might have rigged the hairdryer to fall into the bath? What if Nigel had met someone in Soho and brought him home, knowing that Fr. Justin would be out most of the evening? But, then, whatever happened certainly seemed to be non-malevolent—there was no blood or evidence of violence. The crime lab had indicated that there was no water in the lungs and that there was evidence of cardiovascular effects of an electrical shock, which included acute myocardial necrosis or heart failure. The report also indicated that it is possible that even if the hair dryer was not running it could have sent current into the water. It also noted that although manufacturers make these appliances with a very short, coiled cord—to avoid this very sort of accident—the dryer in question had been augmented with an extension cord, which unfortunately is not an uncommon practice. The Inspector mused that this sounded very similar to what Thomas Merton had suffered when he died while on a convention in Bangkok when he came into contact with an electrical fan, which was not grounded. That, at least, was the conclusion that the press and the authorities had put forward. There was still, it seemed to the Inspector, a number of missing pieces to this puzzle. It was a curious scenario and there were still many things to take into account.

✠

Justin took comfort in reading his evening office at the usual time and thought about Nigel as he recited the psalms. Nigel had often joined in the daily office and some of the thoughts from the office this evening struck a particular chord with Justin. After completing the Office he crossed himself and placed the breviary in its place on the end table near his chair. He was not particularly hungry but thought that he should have something on his stomach as the meeting might go on even longer than usual. He went into the kitchen to see what there was in the refrigerator. Nigel who was rather adept at making soups, had prepared a nice tureen a few days ago, and had frozen some of it. He remembered how he and Nigel had particularly enjoyed it. Another reminder! Justin heated up a bowl of the soup in the microwave and brought out a dinner roll and some Cheddar slices to accompany it. He sat at the kitchen table with his dinner and continued to look over his notes for the evening meeting.

He returned to his favourite armchair in the parlour after his dinner as he had almost an hour to spare before the meeting at half-past seven. He closed his eyes and tried to relax a little, but his thoughts were preoccupied with Nigel and the events of the past three days. He woke up with a start about ten minutes later, confused and realizing that he had drifted off and had some sort of troubled dream. He still had three quarters of an hour before his meeting and so decided to go out for a brief walk to get some fresh air and wake himself from the doldrums. It had sprinkled a little leaving little pools of water on the cars parked in the street but the air was fresh and welcome.

Just before seven thirty he walked through the church to the lounge where most of the group had already gathered. He was immediately approached by Elizabeth who greeted him and exuded concern for her priest and friend.

"How are you holding up, Father?" she said.

"Well, under the circumstances........." his sentence trailing off into nothing.

"We have all heard about Nigel and are deeply distressed."

The others nodded in agreement and solidarity for Father Justin.

They kept a respectful silence as they waited for Father to take his seat in the circle of chairs that had been set up for their discussion and finally everyone had settled down.

"News certainly gets around the parish," Justin remarked, "and I'm sure that we are all devastated, having known Nigel as we did." Supportive nods all around the circle. Justin continued, "It has been quite devastating for me as I've known Nigel for many years—as you have as well—but also because he's been living in the Rectory for these past months and we had grown to know each other on a very personal level. I'm sure you all have many questions about just what actually happened. I too have questions. However, there is a police investigation into the circumstances of Nigel's death and we must allow that to play out without interfering. There certainly are a lot of questions, I can assure you."

"Father," asked Margaret, raising her hand ever so slightly, "This horrible thing raises the old question that people of faith have been asking for ages; Why does God allow such things to happen to people like Nigel, who was always kind and thoughtful and loving?"

"I know Margaret; I ponder over the same thing. You know, on many occasions, and particularly last evening as I was saying my office, my mind was pondering this issue. But, we all know from our everyday experience in life that frequently the wicked go happily on their way abusing the rights of others and the good are left to suffer. There simply is no easy answer, Margaret; we go forward trusting that God is just and loving. I'm at a loss and really can't say anything more than that. But, I completely share your exasperation and frustration with the situation."

The thread was then picked up by Robert, a middle aged widower who had also been a parishioner for many years. He joined in offering some consolation about the subject but basically expressed his view that, although we have deep and complex questions, still we move forward in faith and trust in God's mercy and purpose. Justin nodded in agreement with what Robert had to say and then added: "It does raise the whole question about the power of prayer and how we relate to God, doesn't it! I mean, we continually profess that prayer is an important aspect of our faith, and we always pray for the sick and the needy at Mass. However, I suppose this horrible situation almost forces us to think seriously about how we use prayer. This unfortunate death is, in an odd way, a reminder to us that we should consider our prayer habits. Jesus said that we could move mountains by prayer and the Church throughout the ages has always taught the efficacy of prayer. Jesus' statement about moving mountains and his promise that whatsoever you ask in my name will be granted, perhaps needs to be seen as allegorical and regarded as an assurance that the Father wishes us to cultivate a relationship through prayer. At least, that is one way of looking at it. I don't think any responsible Christian of whatever stripe would ever attempt to use prayer to try and move a mountain. I guess we need to understand our prayer more in the sense of holding up in God's Presence the sick and the troubled as well as the condition of our poor world. It can be dangerous if we begin to think of prayer as giving God ideas that he hadn't thought of, or of trying to manipulate Him. In the Lord's Prayer we say, 'Thy will be done,' and I suppose we need to approach our prayers in light of that. Actually, although this might surprise you, Nigel and I talked about this very subject on several occasions not long ago. He was a remarkably spiritual young man, which is perhaps partly why his death has struck me such a fierce blow. It is actually very much like losing a son."

Margaret chimed in, "I think we all feel that way, Father. It is such a dreadful situation."

The discussion continued on for some time exploring the subject but was always careful to protect Father's sensibilities, as they understood that for him it was much more of a personal situation—akin to losing a family member as Justin explained. Eventually the discussion drew to a conclusion when all the avenues seemed to have been exhausted and the consensus was that, although it was a little earlier than their usual quitting time, they should offer prayers and let Justin return to the Rectory to relax after a taxing day. They were all aware that the investigation would be continuing for some days and perhaps might even last for weeks. Justin bid them good night and left them to tidy things and lock up.

Walking through the darkened church Justin stopped for a moment of reflection before the Blessed Sacrament in the Chapel and to offer another prayer for Nigel. He thought how dead the house seemed now without Nigel's quiet but calming presence. Justin poured a small nightcap of whisky and sat down in his favourite chair to glance over the evening newspaper. After half an hour he turned out lights and went upstairs to his bedroom to begin the evening rituals of preparation for the night. Sleep finally overcame him as he mused on the puzzling events of the past two days.

Five

Justin's morning routine of Mass and correspondence was punctuated with some reading and sermon preparation along with the ubiquitous telephone calls. Mostly the calls were related to parish business but a few of them were from concerned parishioners checking in to see how Father was managing. They were exceptionally thoughtful and cared about the wellbeing of their parish priest. Two of them were kind offers of casseroles and baking for which Justin was extremely grateful. In both cases they would be dropped off at the rectory later in the afternoon.

Justin settled into his comfy sitting room chair at around eleven o'clock with a theological journal. He set the telephone to take messages so that he could devote at least one hour to reading before he put together a sandwich for lunch. It had been arranged that Inspector Ingram and Dr. Landsworth would meet at the rectory at two in the afternoon for their interview.

The Advent readings for Sunday Mass spoke of one *crying in the wilderness* and about *preparing the way of the Lord.* Justin's thoughts were again brought back to his sense of desolation and to how much Nigel's death had made him feel he was in a wilderness helplessly crying out to God for some kind of a response or explanation. As he read on, he wondered just how he was going to approach the texts and present something edifying to his flock. Sometimes, he reflected, it is difficult to see the wider picture when personal issues are so much at the focus of one's thoughts. He realized that usually he was the comforter and the person who consoled and encouraged but that now, he was in need of those comforting words. Usually he had a certain vigour and took delight in preaching but he realized that this week's homily would not be one of his better efforts unless he had some sort of last minute inspiration.

Soon Justin's reverie was broken as he heard the grandfather clock strike noon. A snack might help to evade his mood and the break would perhaps give him a new and brighter frame of mind.

✠

Inspector Ingram arrived at the rectory door just before 2 p.m. struggling to keep control of his brief case and his umbrella, which were being buffeted about, in another rainsquall. Justin took his coat, hat and umbrella and led him into the sitting room. When offered a hot drink the Inspector declined saying that he had just recently finished lunch. They chatted for about fifteen minutes about the investigation as they awaited the arrival of Dr. Landsworth. Justin was noticeably cautious about asking too many questions, as he was quite aware that things were in progress. The Inspector knew full well that Justin was keen to know what progress was being made but was also being restrained by his well-engrained sense of professional confidentiality.

The casual and somewhat awkward conversation was mercifully interrupted by the doorbell. It would surely be Dr. Landsworth. Justin, with a feeling of resignation mixed with frustration, went to open the door. Dr. Landsworth seemed almost eager to step inside and get out of the inclement weather.

John Landsworth was a rather distinguished, lean man perhaps in his sixties wearing rimless glasses and sporting a cravat neatly arranged inside his starched white shirt. Justin shook his hand and said, "John—I'm glad you were able to see the Inspector this afternoon." The Doctor responded, "Thank you, Father. I hope I might be of some assistance, although I can't quite understand how that might be—we shall see. Again, Father, I'm so sorry for all of this mess and the disturbance and anguish it must be for you."

Justin closed the door, took the Doctor's wet overcoat, and placed his umbrella in the stand in the anteroom. He then led Dr. Landsworth into the sitting room and introduced him to the Inspector. He then closed the double doors and as he did so he said, "Gentlemen, I'll leave you to talk. I'll not be far away and will see you off when you are finished."

The Inspector said, "Thank you for coming Dr. Landsworth; I do appreciate it."

"It is no problem Inspector," replied the Doctor, "I'm happy to offer whatever assistance I can in this unfortunate situation."

"Doctor," exclaimed the Inspector, "I'm sure you understand that I needed to interview you since you are one of those who have keys to the Rectory. I'm sure Father has explained all of that to you. And in a short while I'm expecting a constable from our lab to arrive to take the customary fingerprints and do a DNA swab. That is standard procedure in such an investigation—I'm sure you realize that."

"Yes, certainly, Inspector."

"I assume that by now you know that Nigel's body was discovered by Father Justin in his bathtub late on Sunday evening."

"Yes, Inspector, Father has informed me of the events of that evening. And I understand that a hair dryer was dangling in the water."

"That is right, Doctor," said the Inspector and he continued, "I understand that you have known Nigel for some time."

"Yes, Inspector—for perhaps ten or more years."

"Now," continued the Inspector, "Although it appears that this could have been a suicide, the investigation has not been completed. But, could I ask your thoughts about Nigel and his stay here at the Rectory?"

"Certainly, Inspector. Well, first of all, when Nigel became unemployed and needed somewhere to live I thought the idea was a good one—a gesture that was compassionate and quite in keeping with what the Church is all about. I realized that Father was fond of Nigel and appreciated his company. Further, in all the years I've known Nigel I always found him to be a very pleasant and charming person. I could quite understand Father Justin's eagerness to assist Nigel."

"And the possibility that this might have been suicide?" asked the Inspector.

"Well, I'd never have even entertained that idea," responded the Doctor. "I suppose my first thought would probably be that it was an accident."

"I see," retorted the Inspector. He then continued, "Now, I've spoken with one of Nigel's friends—whose name I found on his mobile. In our discussion David was quite upset with the situation but he was very forthright about things, I believe. He intimated that he and Nigel were gay, and although that is neither here nor there, I wonder if you feel that there might have been a—what shall I say—relationship between Nigel and Father Justin?"

"Well, now Inspector," said the Doctor drawing back a little, "I think that it would be inappropriate for me to continue with that line of thought, because as it happens, not only am I involved with this parish in an official capacity, but, more to the point, I'm also Father Justin's personal physician and that would constitute a serious breach of doctor/patient trust, I'm sorry."

"That is no problem, Doctor, I understand completely, and I do appreciate the assistance you have been in sorting through this matter. And, of course, again I value your time in coming here this afternoon. I think the forensic constable may have arrived already, so perhaps we can call Father and get on with things. But, just before I do that, I must ask you where you were on Sunday evening."

"Of course, Inspector, I appreciate that. I was at home with my wife all afternoon and evening."

Graeme noted this in his book and then said, "Thank you Doctor. Perhaps I'll drop by and have a word with her."

"Of course, Inspector."

Graeme moved toward the frosted glass doors, opening one of them and as expected, Justin was not far away. It seems that the constable had arrived and was waiting in the foyer for the interview to conclude.

"Constable Smythe", said the Inspector, "This is Dr. Landsworth and he understands about the routine fingerprinting and DNA swab. Perhaps you could again use the kitchen for that. And Father Justin, I'll be on my way. Doctor, thank you for your co-operation—it is much appreciated."

Justin saw the Inspector out, chatted with him for a few moments at the stoop, and after bidding him goodbye he closed the front door and led Constable Smythe and the Doctor to the kitchen. After about ten minutes they had concluded their work and Justin showed them to the door and after pleasantries bade them farewell.

✠

The press of the crowd in the Underground station was particularly heavy as Inspector Ingram made his way home. He mused that it was partly the rush hour traffic but also that it was the beginning of the weekend for many people. He was not able to squeeze onto the first two trains that lumbered into the Westminster Station but managed to board the third one. It would be a standing commute this evening for certain and he tried to get as near a doorway as possible while still able to hold onto a stanchion and be relatively comfortable. He strained to think above the chatter of a group of schoolgirls and the noise of the car. His mind was still preoccupied with the scene at the Rectory in Sloane Square. His instinct told him that things, for some inexplicable reason, did not seem to be adding up. Nigel, from all accounts so far, did not sound like the sort of person who would take his own life in spite of his employment situation; on the other hand there did not seem to be anyone he had interviewed so far who would have reason or the disposition to do him harm. Nigel appeared to be well respected and admired by everyone. Perhaps there would be some light at the end of the tunnel as the investigation proceeded. He thought to himself, Speaking of tunnels, we are nearing Hampstead and I should be ready to exit momentarily.

It was dark and blustery again as the Inspector approached his building. Checking his post he found nothing of note and proceeded to the lift. It was time for a cocktail as he relaxed and switched on an evening newscast. Eventually, he realized he needed food and went to the refrigerator to see what he could scramble together for dinner. Nothing seemed to appeal to him and he decided to put his hat and coat back on and venture out to a neighbourhood café where he could have something light before attempting to make more telephone calls. He returned to his apartment within the hour and again spread out his papers and diagrams on the dining room table. He still had not managed to contact the remaining two of Nigel's friends. At least he now knew their surnames thanks to David's help, and thought that by now they would have heard the news. He wouldn't likely be shocking them at any rate.

Graeme was lucky this time with his telephone

calls to Jason and Todd. He called Jason first and in a general way explained where the investigation was going. Jason remarked that he had phoned Todd and that, indeed, he also knew of Nigel's death. They agreed that Sunday afternoon would be a possible time to meet together as long as Todd could also be there. Graeme thought he might double up and interview the two young men together as long as they agreed to do that. He said he would be telephoning Todd immediately and would get back to him to confirm a time for a brief meeting at Scotland Yard. They concluded the call and the Inspector rang Todd's number. Todd answered and they chatted for a few moments before the idea of meeting together with Jason on Sunday afternoon was introduced. Todd was agreeable, they decided upon 2:30 p.m. on Sunday, and the Inspector gave instructions as to where his office was located. He then called Jason back and found that his number was engaged. He mused that Todd must have immediately called Jason to discuss the call from Inspector Ingram. Graeme waited about 20 minutes and tried the call again. Jason answered and said that Todd had just called him—a little apprehensive about the meeting but willing to be there. Information about the time and place of the meeting was exchanged and they bade each other goodbye. The Inspector had a feeling that Todd was perhaps a little uncomfortable—probably the idea of dealing with the law.

Again, Graeme studied his notes and schematic diagrams spread out on the dining room table hoping to stumble upon something that he had so far missed. He had done this sort of thing many times before and found that it often led him suddenly to have a bright idea or to notice something that he had previously overlooked. Often such an insight would occur to him and spark a completely new avenue of approach.

Eventually, as the hour approached ten thirty, he abandoned his papers and prepared for sleep. He would be rising very early in the morning to attend the Bishop's Mass at St. John's and he wanted to get a good six hours sleep. No sooner had he placed his glasses on the bedside table, switched off the light and arranged his quilt, and he was soundly asleep.

Six

The alarm clock rang out a shrill reveille at 5:30 and Graeme fumbled in the darkness to stop it. Recollections of the previous day and his schedule of events for Friday immediately flooded back to the forefront of his mind. He rose, straightened the bed covers and put on his bathrobe. A hot shower refreshed and awakened him fully. He dressed and found that there was time to relax for a moment before setting off to the Hampstead station to catch the Tube back into Westminster.

The train was packed even at the early hour of 6:15 am. Inspector Ingram arrived at Sloane Square with only a few minutes to spare before Mass was to begin. He hurried on so as not to be late but when he entered the chapel Bishop Halpin had only moments before gone to the altar, placed the vessels upon it and was opening the missal to find the introit.

.........*"Populus Sion, ecce Dominus veniet ad*

salvandas gentes: et auditam faciet Dominus gloriam vocis suae in laetitia cordis vestre. Qui Regis Israel intende................"

The Bishop's sonorous voice and the pungent, lingering odour of incense and beeswax brought back to Graeme vivid memories of earlier times and of his parish in another part of London. He quietly found a seat near the back and knelt down.

Graeme's thoughts became gradually more focussed as the Mass progressed. Memories of earlier times flashed through his mind—days when he and Mary had regularly gone to Mass with their children. He loved the season of Advent as Justin did —and it brought back to him a sense of the expectation leading up to Christmastide. His thoughts were slightly distracted as he tried to be attentive to the rhythm of the Mass by decisions that he knew he would soon have to make. Should he receive Holy Communion knowing that he had lapsed for some years? Would the Bishop or Justin even know that? He thought to himself that it must have been at Mary's funeral when he last received holy communion.

In his homily the Bishop made a cursory introduction by way of drawing attention to the Gospel reading about "The *blind seeing, the deaf hearing and the lame walking*" and deftly worked that into the issue that was on everyone's mind—the death of the young man whom so many had respected and the overwhelming feeling of disbelief that surrounded it. He recounted the years when he himself had been Rector of St. John's and had watched Nigel as he grew up. His sorrow at Nigel's death was surely as great as anyone's.

Inspector Ingram took particular note of the Bishop's remarks as he would before very long be interviewing him. He conjectured in his mind just how he should approach a Bishop about such a sensitive and personal subject. He pondered whether the usual approach of enquiring about one's whereabouts at the time of the death and opinions about the deceased might not come across as sounding a little improper.

His reverie ended as the Bishop concluded his remarks and continued with the liturgy. His speculations drifted away for the time and he again became engaged in the progression of the Mass. Thoughts of his deceased wife came flooding back to his mind as the Intercessions for the departed were read out. Justin and the Bishop were not the only ones to be reminded of the shortness of life, and Graeme was all of a sudden vividly aware that this was undoubtedly true for almost everyone present on this sombre and dark December morning.

Graeme's thoughts remained fixed upon his departed wife who he missed sorely, especially at moments like this. He was brought back to reality as the Sanctus bells jangled. His thoughts soon returned to Mary as the souls of the Departed were commended to the care of the Almighty during the Canon. When it came time to go forward to receive Holy Communion he no longer had any uncertainty about whether or not it would be appropriate—he simply rose and went to the altar rail confident that this was a matter that involved himself and his God without concern about what others might think; in any case, he rationalized, the notion probably would not even occur to anyone else.

Mass, having ended, the Bishop and server genuflected and left the sanctuary to go to the vestry where they would say the thanksgiving and divest. Following their silent, personal devotions the congregation slowly emptied from the chapel, some of them remaining in the ambulatory to greet one another. After a word or two with one of them, Justin took the arm of Inspector Ingram and led him toward the door to the Presbytery, and in hushed tones explained that Bishop Halpin would soon join them. He reminded the Inspector that the Bishop had been Pastor at St. John's some years ago, knew his way around, and of course that he had a key to the house.

Justin took Inspector Ingram to the sitting room to wait for the Bishop and then put on the kettle. He remarked that he knew the Bishop would probably appreciate a hot drink. Before long he heard the key in the clergy house door and the Bishop let himself in. He placed his coat on a chair in the foyer and entered the sitting room.

"Inspector, nice to meet you finally. I'm Bishop Halpin." The Inspector rose from his chair, extended his hand and greeted the Bishop. "Hello—Graeme Ingram. It is nice to meet you Bishop." The Inspector continued, "Father has just gone to arrange some refreshments and will be back in a moment."

Bishop Halpin and the Inspector exchanged pleasantries for a few moments and soon Justin was back. "I see you have introduced yourselves. Good. Do relax and I'll be back shortly with some tea and muffins. Then I'll leave you to talk." The Bishop was quite relaxed in this atmosphere as he had lived here for some years, although, this morning because of the nature of this meeting he was a little ill at ease. It would perhaps not be such a congenial conversation.

They talked briefly about the usual things; the weather; some city issues and general chitchat. Soon Father appeared again, this time bearing a tray with the tea and pastries. He placed it on the coffee table and enjoined the two to make themselves at home. "I'll leave you gentlemen to talk but I won't be too far away. I expect, Inspector, that the forensic constable will be along soon, and I'll watch for him. "Thank you Father, I appreciate that," responded the Inspector.

Justin closed the French doors leaving them to their interview.

The Inspector began, "Now Bishop Halpin,

before we begin, just a few words of explanation. You understand that it is routine in such investigations that I need to interview you, as you are one of the people who possesses a key to the premises. As we proceed with the investigation we need to be meticulous in following the protocols."

"Yes, Inspector, I do appreciate that."

Graeme was feeling rather uncomfortable about questioning the Bishop. He paused briefly, loosened his tie, and then continued, "Father mentioned the forensic constable who will be joining us later. This is also part of the procedure. He will be taking fingerprints as well as a DNA swab, if you don't mind."

"Certainly, Inspector," rejoined the Bishop, "I've watched enough television dramas to realize what you must do. I do feel a little awkward about the fingerprinting, however, because I'm here quite often and I'm sure my prints are bound to be found somewhere."

"Don't be concerned about that, Bishop," said the Inspector, "we realize your involvement with St. John's."

"Bishop," began the Inspector, "perhaps you could begin by telling me something of your knowledge and acquaintance with Nigel?"

"Certainly, Inspector. Well, when I came to be Rector of St. John's Nigel and his family were parishioners. At that time Nigel was, I suppose, in his early teen years. He was an altar boy and so we often participated together in the liturgy. At that time it was primarily during Sunday Masses. He was a very polite and friendly boy and well liked by everyone in the parish. I cannot think of anyone who did not regard him highly. That is primarily why I do not believe that this tragedy was anything but an unfortunate accident. Nigel had no enemies to my knowledge."

The Inspector interjected, "And what was Nigel's age when you left St. John's and Father Justin came? I presume Fr. Justin followed you."

"Yes, he did follow me, Inspector. And to answer your question, Nigel must have been in his late teens when I left and Father Justin came here. After I became Bishop I continued to be associated with the parish in so much as I was able to say Mass from time to time and to keep contact with friends."

"And in recent times Nigel was living on his own?" asked the Inspector.

"Yes, at some point—I can't remember when exactly-- Nigel's family moved away from London to the north country and Nigel stayed here as he had a job. Then, when his store downsized, Nigel was unemployed and Fr. Justin was kind enough to suggest to him that he come and stay in the Rectory in the interim."

"I see," the Inspector replied. "What about friends? Did Nigel have any close friends?"

"I believe he did, although I've never met any of them," replied the Bishop, "I remember him telling me something about someone, but it has escaped my mind."

"Bishop, I wonder if I might ask you where you were last Sunday afternoon and evening." Inspector Ingram asked.

"Yes, certainly, Inspector. After Mass at the Cathedral I drove up to Oxford to look at antiques. I suppose I left London at around 2 pm. After browsing in my favourite shop, *Magdalen Antiques* and chatting with a middle-aged woman—possibly the owner—I went and enjoyed a pleasant dinner at a restaurant a few doors along. After dinner I strolled around for awhile in the High Street and then drove back to London arriving home at about midnight."

"Do you know the name of the restaurant, Bishop?"

"Yes indeed, it is a very good Italian one called *La Cucina.* It is just a short distance from the antique store at, I believe, 40 St. Clements Road. The antique store is a few doors away, near the intersection with Cowley Road, only steps literally from the Magdalen Bridge."

"Thank you Bishop, that is very helpful," said the Inspector. "I believe that is all I need to ask you Bishop, unless you would like to add anything that might be helpful to solving this mystery."

"No, Inspector, I don't believe I can tell you anything more. I rather doubt if anything I've said will be of much help to you."

"Well, Bishop, let us see if the constable has arrived yet and he will get on with the fingerprinting and DNA swab. It will only take a moment or two of your time and then you can go. And I do thank you for spending your valuable time for this interview. It is much appreciated."

The Inspector opened the doors and they walked into the foyer. Justin was in the adjoining hallway talking with the forensic officer.

"Good," said the Inspector over his shoulder to Bishop Halpin, "This will be quite painless. Father Justin will take you and the constable to the kitchen for this as the fingerprinting can be a little messy and one needs a basin to wash up afterward."

Justin showed them to the kitchen and then returned to bid the Inspector farewell. Graeme thanked Father for organizing meetings and interviews and assured him that perhaps some headway might be made as the investigation proceeded.

Meanwhile, Constable Smythe helped the Bishop get through the messy procedure of fingerprinting and provided some alcohol and paper towels so the Bishop could clean up afterward. He then explained about the DNA swab, which was a simple procedure of getting a swab of saliva on a Q-Tip. Constable Smythe was quite obviously a little tense about the novelty of having to deal with a Bishop and made an awkward comment, just as he went to swab the Bishop's mouth, about doing a *"turn-about"*. They both had a little laugh about it and soon the sample was sealed inside its plastic tube.

Bishop Halpin left the constable in the kitchen to pack away his equipment and went to speak with Justin briefly at the front door before leaving thanking him for the hospitality and making some parting remarks of condolence. He assured Father that he believed the Inspector would soon be able to make a decision or at least draw some conclusion about the mystery of Nigel's death. A car and driver waited outside the Rectory to take Bishop Halpin back to his offices in Westminster. It was slow going through the traffic and the Bishop had ample time to ruminate about how Inspector Ingram's interview had gone. He had felt somewhat uneasy about being questioned and especially fingerprinted, but was rather relieved that it was over and done.

The journey home on the tube was another press of humanity but it was also an opportunity for the Inspector to recall the interviews he had done and to go over the information he had gathered to this point. He was still a little mystified about it all and had the persistent, nagging feeling that there was still a missing piece of the puzzle—something that would perhaps make sense of the mystery. He thought that perhaps his meeting on Sunday with

Jason and Todd might reveal something that had not yet come to light. It seemed that the three young men were rather close friends and therefore may have shared something that would be a lead.

Finally, the train reached Hampstead Station and Graeme managed to push his way through the crowd and exit. As he walked home he planned how he would spend the rest of the afternoon and evening with his charts and notes to be sure he had not overlooked anything—perhaps hoping that he might even stumble across an overlooked clue.

Graeme prepared a light supper consisting of a ham sandwich and a small plate of potato salad as he pored over his notes and charts, which were again spread out over the dining room table. He began by analysing the events as Justin had presented them—slowly, step by step, to see if he could identify anything that might prove to reveal a flaw in the progression of events. He would be speaking with a forensic expert at the Yard on Tuesday to enquire about the hair dryer in the bathtub as it related to the power outage. The autopsy had revealed that there was very little water in Nigel's lungs and that the cardiac arrest was completely consistent with electrocution.

Justin's account of events appeared to match up with the evidence, and there did not seem to be any reason why he might have been involved. He was genuinely distressed by Nigel's death and it troubled him as, indeed, it would trouble any father. Juliana,

Chandler, Dr. Landsworth and the Bishop all seemed to have alibis regarding their movements in the crucial time slot—and in any case, none of them appeared to have any reason or motive to be involved in such a thing.

After considerable time spent going over and over all of the evidence and the contents of the interviews Graeme returned to his papers. As he sat there musing about the people he had interviewed the thought occurred to him that there was still the possibility that Nigel might have taken someone else home with him that evening. What if he met someone at one of those clubs and invited him home for a drink—knowing that Justin would be out until probably quite late? That certainly was a possibility. But somehow, Graeme had the strange feeling that there was something right before his eyes on the table that simply did not add up. He sat for two more hours going over the facts piece by piece— hoping that a new twist might occur to him— something that would steer him perhaps in an unexplored direction.

Eventually, exhaustion overcame him and he decided to relax with a little television news and a nightcap before retiring.

SEVEN

Justin's day began as usual with his early Mass and conversation with some of those who attended Saturday Mass. There was such an immense outpouring of concern for his wellbeing since Nigel's death that it gave him pause to stop and think if he had ever before truly appreciated the sense of family that existed in the parish. In the course of the past week there had been so many telephone calls enquiring about his wellbeing and casseroles appearing at the door that Justin felt truly loved and cared for. He surely realized that he had a loving family. As he contemplated that thought he recalled that he had promised to meet with his sister, June, that afternoon as she wanted to talk with him about a problem with her teenage daughter. He would have to call her and try to fit a visit in with the many other things that he routinely did on Saturdays— including tightening up his thoughts for his sermon for the next day. As well as those things he recalled that he must contact another parishioner who was also dealing with a death in her family.

By the time he had dealt with his visit with June and the extended telephone conversation with the bereaved parishioner, Justin glanced at his watch and discovered that it was already 4:00 o'clock in the afternoon. When he finally had a moment he sat in his study and read his evening office. It was now almost dinnertime and he decided to pour a sherry before making a quick sandwich after which he could sit down and seriously get on with the sermon preparation. All day he had been thinking about just what he wanted to say on Sunday morning. This would be the first Sunday since Nigel's death and he wanted to address the issue since so many in the parish had known Nigel and the extended family had been so very aware of what was happening from day to day since last Monday. He had decided that the readings for Sunday's Mass would form the basis for his remarks as was the usual practice, and found that there was a logical and appropriate way of weaving his remarks about Nigel into it. He had a quiet chuckle about that as he remembered a conversation with a fellow priest when they had both noted that it was actually possible to weave almost any issue into a sermon if one put one's mind to it.

✠

Inspector Ingram had decided to use Saturday as a day off as he had been working on the case with unrelenting fervour all week. He slept in an hour or so more than his usual rising time and had a leisurely breakfast around nine o'clock. Then, after a shower, he returned to the dining room table where his charts and notes were spread out to have another look at the puzzle.

Graeme took his pad and pencil and made some notes in preparation for his visit to the antique shop in Oxford on Monday and for his meeting with the criminologist on Tuesday when they would discuss the results of the autopsy. He had thought of a number of points that would need to be raised with each of them. There was also the meeting on Sunday afternoon with Todd and Jason, and although it would probably be rather simple and routine Graeme wanted to confirm a few points with them and hear any new information that they may be able to offer.

✠

At mid-afternoon Todd went to his telephone, picked up the receiver and poised to dial Jason—he hesitated; returned the receiver and leaned against the wall considering what he was about to suggest to Jason. Was what he was going to suggest really of such concern? Or was he just being paranoid. He remained there for a few moments debating with himself. Finally he went ahead and dialled Jason. The phone rang quite a number of times and he thought that perhaps Jason was out. Just as he was about to hang up Jason answered, "Hello! Jason here!"

"Hi Jason, it's Todd. How are you doing?"

"I'm fine, and you?"

Todd replied, "Well, I have an idea that I want to run past you. Instead of the usual Saturday night clubbing I wondered if you and David would like to come to my apartment for drinks and perhaps we could talk a bit about our meeting tomorrow afternoon with Inspector Ingram. As you know, I had a bit of a run-in with the police a few years ago and I'm frankly, a little uneasy about this meeting."

"I understand your concern Todd—but to answer your question, or rather, suggestion, it would be fine with me. Why don't you contact David and run it past him and if that is agreeable then just set a time and get back to me."

"Thanks, Jason. I'll do that. And I hope it will work out. I'll call David and see what he thinks and then get back to you."

"Alright Todd—go ahead with it and I'll wait for your call to confirm it. I'm in for the rest of the day —so bye for now."

"Bye Jason. Talk to you a little later."

Todd was able to reach David within minutes of talking with Jason and David thought it would be fine. They chose a time to get together and Todd called Jason back right away to give him the news. They had decided to meet together at Todd's place at eight o'clock that evening. Todd had assured each of them that he would provide the drinks and some cheese and crackers.

✠

David, Todd and Jason were all in their mid-twenties as Nigel had also been and they were quite similar in their appearance and manner. They were all rather trendy—dressed neatly and were fashion conscious—no surprise that they found each other compatible. Todd was a little more contemporary than the other two and had a couple of piercings, which may have been why he had the altercation with a constable outside one of the Pimlico clubs. Perhaps that coupled with his tendency to jump to conclusions quickly made him appear to be somewhat aggressive. The three of them, with Nigel, had met at various times through socializing and had become quite close. They had enjoyed dinners out or at each other's flats on many occasions as well as the Saturday nights clubbing. They had all felt that it wouldn't really be appropriate to try and do so at the Rectory mainly because it might have put Justin in a somewhat awkward position. Justin was, however, a rather sociable person who probably would have enjoyed it. The young men were more than likely trying to save themselves from awkward moments in the company of a priest.

As eight o'clock approached Todd was busy preparing nibblies and setting up his bar. He had spent some time earlier dusting and tidying up magazines and papers so that the sitting room was comfortable for their quiet evening. Soon the doorbell rang and it was David who arrived a few minutes early. Todd met David at his door and welcomed him in taking his jacket and umbrella. Putting the umbrella in a stand in the hallway Todd took David's new leather jacket and after admiring it and discussing the new purchase, he placed it on the bed. David went into the sitting room while Todd poured him his usual gin and tonic. David walked over to the large aquarium that was Todd's pride and joy. After looking at it for a few minutes he called over his shoulder to Todd who was in the kitchen, "What happened to those cute neon fish? Are they hiding in the grass?" From the kitchen Todd called out, "Oh, the neon tetras! I don't really know David —they just seem to have vanished. I haven't seen them for a week. The woman at the pet shop told me that they could co-exist with the other fish—but I somehow doubt it. I think that big angelfish ate the two of them. I won't get any more fish that small."

Todd came back into the sitting room with their drinks—passed David his gin and motioned to him to have a seat on the chesterfield. They chatted for a few minutes catching up on news when almost immediately the doorbell rang and Jason was at the entranceway. Todd let him into the building and soon he was knocking on the door. As Jason entered the flat and took off his coat he remarked to Todd that this was a nice idea and that they would be able to have a nice quiet conversation for a change. Entering the sitting room David greeted Jason and gave him a hug. "So good to see you Jason. It seems like forever for some reason—perhaps the events of the past week," David remarked.

"Yes, it has been a horrible time, hasn't it?"

"Well, Jason," Todd interjected, "What would you like to drink—your usual Pimm's?" "Yes, that would go down nicely," David answered.

Todd left the two to talk while he got Jason's drink. They seated themselves being careful to leave Todd's favourite chair vacant.

"So, how have you been dealing with all of this David?" Jason asked. "I understand the Inspector found your number on Nigel's mobile. It must have been a surprise to receive a call from Scotland Yard."

"That is for sure," rejoined David. "I had heard about Nigel's death on the grapevine and only half believed it, but then when the inspector called it really hit home. It has been a bad week for sure and I feel just sick about Nigel—as I know you two do."

Todd returned with Jason's Pimm's and his own drink, handed Jason his, and sat down. "Well," he said, raising his glass, "here's to poor Nigel, wherever he is!" The three friends sipped a libation to their friend and sat solemnly for just a moment.

Jason was the first to break the silence. "So David, what do you make of all of this since you have already had an interview with Inspector Ingram? Do you really think Nigel topped himself as some seem to think?" David thought for a moment and then responded, "Well, first of all the Inspector was careful to point out to me that the investigation was in progress and that no conclusions have been made yet. And as for my thoughts—well, I really have no reason to believe that Nigel would have done that. At least, he never indicated to me that he was concerned or troubled about anything. He seemed always to be in very good spirits and I don't think he would have hidden some dark secret from me." Jason nodded in agreement with David's assessment, and then asked, "How could he possibly have accidentally knocked the hair dryer from its cradle and into the tub. It must have been horrible!"

Todd interjected at this point, "But what if someone else was there in the house at the time and there was monkey business? You don't think that Father Justin could have done it!"

"I can't imagine that. I always had the impression that they rather liked each other. I know that Nigel had hinted that Father possibly fancied him, but he actually made it clear that their friendship was Platonic. If I'm not wrong I had the impression that Nigel was attracted to older gentlemen, but in any case, I hardly think that Father Justin would have dreamed of harming him."

David added, "From my interview with the Inspector I got the impression that in addition to talking with us he was interviewing everyone who had keys to the church buildings and the Rectory. I'm not quite sure who they are, but it sounds like they are checking out every possibility. Of course, I suppose it is possible that Nigel met someone and took him home, but I rather doubt that. It certainly wouldn't be the Nigel I knew."

"You both know that I've a bit of an awkward feeling toward the police," Todd exclaimed, "since that scuffle I had outside that club in Pimlico one Saturday night. How did you find the Inspector's.....ummm....attitude when you talked with him. I'm assuming that he does realize that there is a gay element in all of this."

"Yes, he does," David added. "When he began asking about my association with Nigel I felt comfortable to reveal that we often went clubbing on many Saturday evenings. I simply mentioned Soho and Pimlico and he immediately made a reference to the *Clipper* so I knew that he was quite up to speed on such things—and he seemed to be completely easy about it. When I think back I believe he was even savvy about the *Enclave* in Brewer Street, so I doubt that there is any difficulty with that. He is pretty worldly-wise I think."

David continued, "Listen, I don't think you two have anything to worry about at your meeting with the Inspector tomorrow afternoon. He is very nice and who knows, you might remember something that will be important in this investigation. I know it all seems rather a mystery to us, but perhaps there is more to what the Inspector has discovered which, of course, he can't talk about. Let's just hope that the mystery is solved. In any case, Nigel is gone and there's nothing we can do about that. I imagine that there will be a funeral eventually once the police have concluded their work and poor Father Justin and everybody can have some closure. I gather that the parish has been quite stunned by it all."

The three talked on for hours reminiscing about Nigel. As their drinks began to hit home the conversation mellowed and turned from the tragically morbid into a somewhat pleasant and nostalgic remembrance of their friend.

EIGHT

Inspector Ingram, an early riser, awoke around eight o'clock on Sunday morning in spite of the fact that he had much of the day off. After bathing and dressing he settled into his *Sunday Telegraph*—all part of his morning ritual. He had noticed in Saturday's paper that Bishop Halpin would be preaching at the Cathedral today and thought that he would attend now that he had broken the ice. He was also curious to observe the Bishop again and to get a sense of his personality and demeanour. That was still a few hours off so he took the opportunity to go through notes and jottings one more time. The case of Nigel Black had dominated his thoughts for the entire week.

Graeme also wanted to review the notes of his interview with David and prepare to meet with Todd Marshall and Jason Grant later in the afternoon. They had been kind enough to meet on a Sunday, as they were both free. It had been decided that they would come to the Yard offices.

As ten o'clock struck on the grandfather clock in the Ingram's hallway the Inspector was putting his coat and hat on in preparation for the trip into town to go to Mass. He arrived in plenty of time and after arranging his coat in the corner of the pew he knelt down and said his preparatory prayers. When he finished, he sat back and perused the pew leaflet for a few minutes and then looked upward and admired the intricacy of the ceiling and arches as a meditative organ voluntary echoed throughout the vast building.

The Mass began promptly at 11:00 am. Graeme felt good being back at church. He hadn't realized that so many fond memories were hidden there in the smells, sounds and imagery, which were conjured up by the words of the liturgy. Eventually, Bishop Halpin ascended the steps to the pulpit and when the music died away he began: *"In the Name of the Father, and of the Son, and of the Holy Spirit. Amen.*

Bishop Halpin began with a quote from the Gospel reading for the Third Sunday of Advent, which was a question that was put to John the Baptist. "Who are you? Are you the one who is to come?" The Bishop went on to expound how John confessed that he was not the Christ; that he was unworthy even to untie His sandal; that he was merely preparing the way for the Christ. The sermon went on to deal with the issues involved in being in positions of leadership in the church and in society and yet still retaining a sense of humility. He tried to explain how difficult that can be—and how delicate a balance it is especially in the life of the church and particularly for a Bishop. He talked about how many people seem to have the idea that the priesthood is such a glamorous vocation— whereas for most of the time it is slow and plodding work. He remarked how people generally see the clergy in church at the centre of the action and in the midst of glorious worship and music—but rarely see them struggling and agonizing with distraught people trying to cope with illness or personal failures.

Graeme had the distinct feeling that the Bishop was trying to pour out something of himself in his analysis. He thought to himself that *is* after all, precisely what a good Priest endeavours to do in proclaiming Christ's Gospel. The Inspector felt a palpable empathy for Bishop Halpin and was moved by his genuine pastoral concern. He radiated a sensitivity for everything that is deeply spiritual and yet at the same time was clearly aware of the realities of the every-day world. Graeme found his thoughts wandering toward memories of his wife and family—the very sacredness of life—and his devotion to the search for truth and justice in his work.

After the Mass Graeme went to the crypt where some of the parishioners gathered for refreshments and became engaged in conversation with several interesting people including a colleague whom he had not seen for some years.

✠

Todd met Jason at a prearranged location on Broadway shortly before 2:30 p.m. and began their search for the entranceway the Inspector had mentioned. They soon found themselves on the third floor and discovered where the Inspector's offices were. Graeme had left the outer door open and was waiting just inside. He was impressed that they were so punctual. They went through the outer office and into the Inspector's working office. He asked them to be seated and to relax assuring them that this would probably not be a very long meeting. Graeme began by offering them coffee, which one of the staff had brought. They both answered in the affirmative so Graeme poured three cups.

"Perhaps you would like to fix the coffee to your own liking," he suggested. "There is cream and sugar here on this shelf." Once re-seated, the Inspector continued, "I want to thank you both for coming in on a Sunday afternoon; it is much appreciated. So, as background, you both know, I'm sure, that Nigel was found by Father Justin in a bathtub late last Sunday evening having apparently had an accident involving a hair dryer. He was pronounced dead by the constables who attended shortly after Father Justin called the precinct. I suppose that you heard about it within a day or so."

Jason replied, "Yes I heard about it from David who had received your phone call. He had already heard about it somehow and was extremely shocked when his call display showed that the call was from Nigel."

The Inspector continued, "Yes, that was unfortunate, but I had to begin somewhere and it was a stroke of luck that we found the mobile. That enabled us to contact you and also Nigel's parents.

"Inspector," Todd asked, "do you know what actually happened? I mean was it an accident or was it suicide. I gather that some have been wondering about that."

"That, I'm afraid, is still a bit of a mystery," added the Inspector, "which I thought perhaps you might be able to shed some light on. Do either of you know of any problems or worries that might have pushed Nigel to doing something that drastic?"

Jason began, "Nigel was, in my estimation, very together and happy about his life. He appreciated being able to stay at the Rectory and felt good about that. I don't know of any problem that would drive him to do something that drastic—it simply isn't like Nigel." Todd nodded in agreement and said, "That's right—Nigel was the epitome of a well grounded person. He never spoke of anything that might be a serious issue in his life. He was constantly working at finding employment, felt badly that his store had downsized, but he was very happy at the Rectory and he was very grateful to Father Justin—and I'm told that the two of them got on very well, and enjoyed each other's company."

The Inspector scratched his head as he listened and nodded when Jason remarked about the congenial aspects of life at the Rectory. "That is what everyone has said, Jason, which still leaves me in a quandary I'm afraid. It does appear that this might have been simply an accident—but something about it urges me to look more carefully at the situation." He continued, "Now, you undoubtedly know that David and I spoke about all of this a few days ago."

"Yes," they both responded in chorus.

"Well, I'm sure you both know where our conversation went!"

Again, in unison they nodded.

"Well," the Inspector wondered aloud, "Then we all know where we are coming from—so perhaps we can just jump right into the middle of things! Do you think that it could be possible that Nigel met someone and took him home and then things went dreadfully wrong? Please forgive me, but we simply have to consider every possibility here," the Inspector added.

Todd was first to respond, "I don't think so Inspector, I just can't picture that. Nigel was very particular and guarded. It simply wouldn't be in his nature to do that. Especially, taking someone he had just met home to the Rectory. I haven't even been there myself and I've known Nigel for some years. No, he would never have done that."

Jason added, "Yes, I agree with Todd, Inspector, that would just be too far fetched—not the Nigel we knew."

"And what about Father Justin," the Inspector asked, "I understand he might have been, shall we say, *keen* on Nigel?"

"Oh Inspector," gasped Todd theatrically, "you have been doing your homework! Well, seriously now, yes, we believe that was true—according to Nigel—but I doubt that Father would have done anything to harm him. Nigel liked older gentlemen, to be honest, and Father Justin was not quite old enough. And anyway, they had a wonderful friendship, which was quite deep and Platonic. No, I didn't believe for a minute that Father Justin would in any way be involved in this horrible affair. I certainly hope not—that would surely be a scenario that would even shock what little faith I have."

"Well, gentlemen," the Inspector exclaimed, "I do appreciate your thoughts and willingness to come here. You have been very helpful—and I see that I still have some way to go in solving all of this. I'll see you out—and again, many thanks! We'll get to the root of this in time."

Graeme walked down to the main floor and showed the young men out thanking them again for their insight and cooperation.

NINE

Graeme rose early on Monday morning so as to get a grip on what was going to be a busy day. After a light breakfast of a boiled egg and some toast and jam he dressed and prepared to wrestle with the rush hour traffic and the crowded train from Hampstead to Westminster and the Yard offices. His jottings and schematic diagrams had been left at the office and he thought that he might spend the morning going over them yet again with the hope of making some sort of breakthrough. The afternoon would be spent on his visit to Oxford to see what he could confirm with the staff at the antique store.

The trains were indeed packed at 7:30 a.m. and it proved to be another stand-up journey for the Inspector. Thousands of commuters poured out from the underground in Westminster on their way to offices and shops. Graeme's walk to Scotland Yard was refreshing as the sky had cleared somewhat and he was glad of the fresh air—or mostly fresh air, as the acrid smell of diesel fumes from cabs occasionally invaded his nostrils. He had a brief conversation with a colleague when he entered the Yard building and then proceeded up to the third floor and to his office. Some good soul had put a pot of fresh tea in his office. After hanging up his coat he was able to pour a cup and attend to messages, which had come in since yesterday. Nothing particularly urgent there. He was able to get on with the mass of papers spread out on his desk.

Graeme became lost in his thoughts as he puzzled with this mystery. The interview with Todd and Jason had not opened any new doors for him. Their views and thoughts only confirmed what he already knew from the previous interviews—that Nigel was a highly respected and pleasant young man. He mused how it always seemed to be so much easier to get at the truth of situations when the main characters were disagreeable or deceitful. Perhaps, after all, this case was truly just a matter of a simple accident.

It was now getting on toward noon and Graeme thought about getting a sandwich from the café next door and poring over his notes for one last time before setting off for the train to Oxford. He took the stairs to the main floor and soon found a roast beef sandwich that appealed to him and took it along with a fruit juice to the checkout. Back upstairs to his office for one more perusal of the papers and notes before going to Paddington Station to leave for

Oxford. Again, as he looked over the notes, he felt as though he was drawing a blank with respect to Nigel Black. He had that odd feeling again that there was a piece of the puzzle which was missing, yet ever so close—if only he could unearth it.

Graeme took a cab to Paddington and soon had his return ticket to Oxford in hand. His timing was just right and he found that his train would be leaving in about 10 minutes. The train was waiting in its platform; he found his car immediately and settled into his seat. It quickly began to fill up as he looked through his brief case for some reading material. It had been quite some time since Graeme had been outside of Metropolitan London and he was keen to see a bit of the green countryside through Berkshire and Oxfordshire. He enjoyed rail travel and the hour-long trip was quite pleasant. The farmland and pastures brought back memories of his boyhood and his thoughts travelled to times long past. He was on a direct, fast train but he caught flashing glimpses of the signs indicating Slough and Reading. Before he knew it they were beginning to slow as the train rumbled through the endless mass of rail lines leading into Oxford Station. The wheels clicked ever more and more slowly as they passed over spur lines—the coach lurching and groaning occasionally. They finally, after a faint screech, came to a full stop and the passengers began to gather up coats and bags and prepare to leave the coaches.

✠

The weather had remained pleasant all day with partially cloudy skies so Graeme decided to take a stroll from the station to the antique shop on St. Clements Road. As the Bishop had noted, the shop is itself called St. Clements Antiques. The stroll was pleasant and Graeme thought to himself that this was just what he needed after the trip from London. He soon found his way to the Magdalen Bridge and St. Clements Road was just a little beyond. He had taken the trouble to consult a map before leaving the Yard and had a rather good idea of just where things were situated.

The Inspector checked his breast pocket to be sure he had the photo of Bishop Halpin, which he had found in a newsletter at the back of the Cathedral. He soon spotted the antique shop sign and headed for the door. He entered to the sound of a clanking cowbell. There did not seem to be anyone around as he browsed the array of interesting furniture and other treasures. Soon, from a back room, emerged a genteel looking woman with carefully coiffed grey hair and a necklace of huge amber beads. She approached Graeme and greeted him. "Good afternoon—welcome to St. Clements."

Graeme responded, "Good afternoon. How are you?"

"Fine," she replied, "can I help you?"

Graeme thought to himself how this lady

reminded him of an aunt who had been a university professor. She seemed very articulate and spoke confidently with a cultured accent. He imagined that she must be quite an expert in 18th Century furniture, which seemed to be mostly what this shop specialized in as Bishop Halpin had mentioned.

"I'm Inspector Graeme Ingram, from Scotland Yard in London."

She said, "Welcome Inspector, I'm Elizabeth Dafoe. How may I help you?"

He continued, "I'm wondering if you might be able to assist me with a case I'm working on."

"Well, Inspector, I certainly will if I can, although I can't quite imagine how." She asked the Inspector if he could excuse her for just a moment and she returned to the back room from which she had emerged. In a moment she came back with her husband and introduced him to Graeme.

"Inspector, this is my husband George—George, Inspector Ingram from Scotland Yard. The Inspector wants to chat with me George so could you just mind the store for a bit in case anyone comes in. The Inspector and I'll talk in the back room to have a little privacy."

"Of course, Elizabeth—and welcome to our shop Inspector," George responded.

"Right this way Inspector," Elizabeth said, moving aside the curtain. The room was cluttered with knickknacks and curios. In the far corner were two stuffed chairs. "Do have a seat Inspector," she motioned toward the chairs and they sat down.

Graeme continued, "I'm working on an investigation and I'm wondering if you perhaps have seen this gentleman?" He brought out the photo of the Bishop and showed it to her.

She looked it over momentarily and said, "Yes, Inspector, I do recognize him. He has browsed here on a number of occasions before and in fact I saw him about a week ago. Strange you know—he has always appeared in civvies until that last time when he came in wearing clerical attire. He seemed to be making a point of introducing himself and telling me his name—Bishop Halpin, if I remember correctly?"

"That's right," added Graeme.

"Is there some problem, Inspector?" she exclaimed, wide eyed and furrowing her brow.

"Not necessarily, this is a routine investigation and we are merely checking out some details."

"Oh," she said, with a tone of relief.

"I'm wondering just when you might have seen him," Graeme continued.

She replied thoughtfully, "I believe it must have been a week ago today—or perhaps it was the Saturday before that."

"Are you sure it might not have been a week ago Sunday?"

"No Inspector," she replied, "You see we aren't open on Sundays."

"Oh really," he said with a questioning inflection. He paused for a moment and then added,

"Then, can you remember whether it was Saturday or Monday?

She thought for a moment and then added, "It surely must have been Monday, because I recall George was here and he does not come in on Saturdays as he is occupied with something else then."

"Thank you so much," the Inspector remarked, "You have been very helpful indeed."

"I do hope there is nothing serious about all of this. Is the Bishop alright, then?" she asked.

"Yes Mrs. Dafoe, he is fine, this is just a routine investigation about another situation. And thank you so much again, I'm very grateful," he added, before leaving the shop.

"Very well, Inspector, I hope I've been of some assistance."

"You have indeed; thank you again and good afternoon."

Graeme opened the door to leave again to the clanking of the cowbell. He stood in front of the shop looking at the Bishop's picture in his hand and trying to make some sense of that bit of information. Surely, he thought, there must be some sort of confusion in Mrs. Dafoe's recollection of the sequence of events. He walked a few yards on and found the Italian restaurant but discovered that it was closed. He walked back toward the High Street, his mind in a quandary trying to assess this new twist. It was getting late in the afternoon and he decided to walk directly to the station and take the next available train back to Paddington. It was not a long wait and before he knew it he was back on the train still contemplating his visit to the antique shop. It was still not adding up, he thought, and perhaps it is even becoming more bizarre than ever.

The train eased into the maze of spurs in the Paddington yard and Graeme was soon making his way along the platform and through the station to the street. Arriving home at shortly after 6:30, he poured a scotch and looked over his mail—wincing at the volume of advertising fliers—before checking the refrigerator to see what things he could find to pull together to make a light supper. There was bread and cheese as well as some left over stew, which he thought, might make a pleasant dinner. He brought out the things he would need and neatly organized them on the counter space. Graeme mused to himself how odd it was that leftovers frequently taste better the second time around.

After a satisfying meal he again looked over his notes and diagrams. Now he was trying to adjust his thinking with regard to the comments and information that Elizabeth Dafoe had provided. Curious, he thought! Could she perhaps have been wrong about which day the Bishop visited her shop? He was abundantly aware how the recollections of witnesses can be remarkably inaccurate. There were certainly many questions still to be addressed. He had the impression that the case was still going in all directions and that nothing very conclusive had emerged. He knew that in this work one must persist until something concrete comes into view, which it usually did, given enough time. Perhaps his meeting with the pathologist tomorrow might reveal some clues or at least shed more light on things so that a different course of action might be taken.

The Inspector felt the need for an early night as the day had been somewhat tiring and his thoughts about it were reinforced as he heard the grandfather clock in the hallway strike ten. He finished sorting out the papers he wanted to take with him in the morning for his meeting with the pathologist, arranged them neatly in his briefcase, and put out lights before making his way upstairs to prepare for sleep.

TEN

Graeme's commute into Central London was particularly problematic this morning. For starters the crowds waiting to board built up and there was a huge backlog. The trains simply seemed not to be running. Normally, there was a departure at least every few minutes but Graeme had now been standing there in the cold for well over half an hour. A rumour began to circulate through the crowd that there had been another jumper somewhere along the line—what is flippantly called a *"one under"*. The Inspector glanced at his watch repeatedly as he stood waiting. There was not much one could do about it, however. He had an appointment that morning with Dr. Evans, the pathologist, in his offices on the sixth floor and hoped that he was not going to be late for it. He was eager to see the pathology and autopsy reports and to discuss the findings with Dr. Evans.

After a wait of another fifteen minutes the first

train slowly pulled into the station and people scrambled to board. It was only minutes before the first train was packed and it left the station. Within minutes another arrived, filled and was on its way. The Inspector finally managed to board the third train and finally he was on his way to Westminster.

Now he felt a little comfort knowing that he would be able to keep his appointment. He had managed to find a seat this trip and sat with his brief case on his lap which he opened slightly and withdrew a few documents so as to review the questions he wanted to ask Dr. Evans. His thoughts were preoccupied with questions about Nigel's being found in the bath and how exactly the hair dryer happened to fall from its bracket. He was also still trying to understand the conversation with Mrs. Dafoe and wondered whether or not her recollection was accurate.

Graeme finally returned the papers and closed the brief case as they were approaching the station where he wanted to get off. He managed to push through the crowd to position himself near a door. There was a good deal of movement as many people were now nearing their work places so he had no difficulty. When the train reached his stop he was soon on his way up the escalator and onto the street a short walk from the Yard building. There would still be time to unpack his papers before taking the lift to the sixth floor.

Just before ten o'clock Graeme tidied the papers

and notes on his desk before visiting the pathologist. He glanced over the jottings he had made with reference to the autopsy reports and placed them in his breast pocket, stared idly for a moment or two out onto the busy street, then left his office and walked to the lift.

Graeme found Dr. Evans sitting at his desk occupied with a telephone call. He saw Graeme enter and motioned to come in and have a seat—that he would be finished momentarily. The Inspector stood for a few minutes perusing the shelves of medical and scientific journals and textbooks. Before long Dr. Evans concluded his conversation, stood and walked around his desk extending his hand to Graeme.

"Good morning, Inspector. Punctual as usual, I see."

Graeme shook his hand and responded, "Well, I didn't want to keep you waiting—and, after all, it is only a few yards away from my office. How are you keeping, Doctor?"

"Quite well, Inspector, and you?"

"Busy, as usual; particularly with this case. I'll be rather interested to see what the forensic team has discovered and to see the autopsy reports."

Reaching back to his desk, Dr. Evans retrieved a large manila envelope with the Inspector's name on it and passed it to Graeme. He then suggested that they sit down and discuss any particular queries that Graeme might have.

Dr. Evans began, "These reports are quite lengthy which is usual—about 32 pages in all I believe—and I'm sure you will be able to synthesize them with the information you've gleaned from your investigation. As usual, the references to fingerprints and DNA samples are coded with numbers and I've attached the usual page at the end giving a key as to whom they refer."

"Thank you, Doctor, I'll be most interested to read this material. I do have a question or two for you, however. Undoubtedly, they will be answered in the reports but I'd just like to share them with you if you have a few moments."

"Surely, Inspector—go ahead."

"Well, first off, I was wondering about the likelihood that the hair dryer in the bath could have caused the death, and secondly, might the death have been by drowning?"

"Well, as to your second question first—the autopsy report indicates that there was little or no water in the lungs, so that would rule out drowning. As to your first question about the hair dryer—the autopsy did confirm that the cause of death was cardiac arrest and the hair dryer falling into the bath could certainly have caused that. However, I realize that that alone does not really prove anything. They manufacture those appliances with very short cords to prevent this sort of thing happening. But, people, not realizing the danger, persist in adding extension cords to them for the sake of convenience. And this dryer did have an extension cord attached to it. I'm afraid that even given that information there might still remain a mystery—and that, Inspector, puts it back in your court, I'm afraid."

"Yes, I can see that, Doctor. But, as you said earlier, the findings of the autopsy and the other elements of the criminology report together with our investigation might shed some light on the matter. I'll just have to settle down and give these reports a good read and see what we can come up with."

"I'm sure things will gradually come together with the material you have gathered in your investigation, Inspector," added Doctor Evans.

"I certainly hope so," Graeme remarked. "Thank you so much for your time—it is much appreciated.

Dr. Evans showed Graeme to the door—shook his hand, wished him well and bid him goodbye. Graeme returned to his office with what he hoped would lead to the solving of this mystery tucked protectively under his arm.

✠

Graeme put the autopsy reports to the side of his large oak desk and began to deal with some other important correspondence and interoffice work that had accumulated.

It would be best, he thought, to clear that away first so that he could concentrate on plodding through the voluminous report. Some of the issues scattered in amongst the correspondence could be dealt with on the telephone and he spent a good hour making calls. The nature of this work was simply that projects and issues go on forever, and usually with numbers of cases open and being worked on simultaneously. He recalled how, when he began in this office he had been initially overcome with anxiety as he tried to juggle all of those balls at the same time. He soon learned that he could—with a careful system of notes and calendars—manage to keep up with the various threads without neglecting or forgetting about any of them. On occasion a particular case might for a time seem to be particularly urgent and need his full attention. At this moment the case of Nigel Black and St. John's was definitely at the top of Graeme's priority list and needed his complete attention.

Before embarking on the long and detailed read he would need some lunch, as it was now almost noon. He went down to the sandwich shop on the ground floor to see if he could get another of those succulent roast beef sandwiches he had found the other day. He also picked up a small bottle of fruit juice to accompany the sandwich. The attendant made a fresh sandwich for him to his specifications and with Dijon mustard for which he had a special partiality. Then, back to the office to begin combing through the reports. The secretary was happy to take messages or to defer any telephone calls so that the Inspector could immerse himself in the reports without interruption.

Graeme closed the office door, retrieved the manila envelope containing the reports and settled himself into his easy chair, placing his lunch on the small table at his side. Before delving into the reports he spent a few minutes simply enjoying the sandwich. That finished, he opened the sealed envelope eager to see what information it might reveal to assist in solving the mystery. These reports are of course written up in the jargon of investigative criminology, which Graeme had become quite adept at deciphering. They are always very carefully drafted so as not to evaluate or arrive at conclusions—that was Graeme's department.

The first section dealt with the coroner's findings and were concerned mostly about what Graeme and Dr. Evans had discussed—namely, the observation that little water was found in Nigel's lungs and that there was definite evidence of cardiac arrest. There were no other marks or injuries on the body, which indicated that there certainly had not been any kind of struggle or even a fall in the bathtub. The water in the tub was still slightly warm when the forensics people arrived which would indicate that in all probability whatever happened took place fairly late in the evening—perhaps at about ten in the evening on Sunday.

The forensic report dealing with fingerprints revealed nothing particularly conclusive. As one would expect, prints for Justin and Nigel were found in many locations throughout the clergy house. The prints belonging to Juliana and Chandler were discovered mainly in the kitchen and on some door handles. On the kitchen sideboard there were prints matching all of these people, which was to be expected, especially on coffee mugs and water glasses. The Bishop's prints were also found; but as he himself had pointed out, that was to be expected, as he was a frequent visitor to the Rectory. There did not appear to be any unidentifiable fingerprints. That does not reveal anything particularly odd, Graeme thought—the prints all belonged to people who had keys to the house and furthermore, unidentifiable prints could introduce a considerable obstacle into the investigation. The exact placement of these prints did raise somewhat of a question in Graeme's mind—he would have to think on it. One particular piece of information did cause him to raise his eyebrows.

Graeme managed to digest all of the information in the reports by about 2:30 in the afternoon. He closed the folder—leaned back in the comfortable, high backed chair, and appeared to be dozing. He needed time to think and mull over all the information that was contained in the forensic and autopsy reports and decide what he would do next. It seemed inevitable to him that he was going to have to make an extremely difficult decision. His thoughts flashed back to the various interviews he had conducted during the past eight days—reaching back to gain an understanding of how they might now be interpreted in light of the forensic reports. He remained in what seemed like a trance for the longest time agonizing over the situation. Everything seemed to be falling into place for the Inspector now, except that it appeared that there would be one fairly awkward issue he would have to confront. He pondered it for a time and then decided that he must simply wade in and take action. He needed to talk with Bishop Halpin again.

He rose, placed the forensic materials on his desk, picked up the phone, and placed a call to the Diocesan Offices. A secretary answered. Graeme said, "Hello. This is Inspector Ingram of Scotland Yard. I wonder if I might speak to Bishop Halpin."

"Just a moment, Inspector," she replied, "I'll see if he is available."

"Thank you," he responded as he was put on hold. After a brief pause, she came back on and said, "I'll put you through Inspector." Almost immediately the Bishop answered, "Hello Inspector, how are you?"

"Fine, Bishop. I'm wondering if I might drop by your office sometime tomorrow to talk."

"I believe so, Inspector. Just let me check my book." After a shuffling of pages and mutterings, the Bishop said, "Would ten o'clock be suitable for you Inspector?"

"Yes, that would be fine Bishop, I'll be there at

ten."

"I'll look forward to seeing you Inspector, good-bye."

✠

Graeme spent the rest of the afternoon dealing with paper work and tidying up files pertaining to cases he was working on which had become side tracked recently. He made his way through the rush hour crowds and stopped at the butcher shop near his home to buy a steak to grill for dinner. Upon arriving home, he first poured himself a large scotch. He then began to peel a potato, which he sectioned and placed in a saucepan of water and placed it on a back burner. A little later, after a scan of the newspaper on the dining room table, Graeme went back to the sideboard to prepare broccoli, which he also put on the stove in a saucepan with a collapsible steamer. As he waited, he sat down for a moment in the den and watched part of the evening newscast as he sipped his scotch. Always tragic and violent news, he thought to himself, it does get to one. He tried to eradicate Nigel Black from his thoughts even for a few moments, but was not really having much success. Finally, he switched the television off and returned to the kitchen to deal with dinner. The vegetables were nearly done now and it was time to put the steak into the frying pan and quick-grill it. While the steak was on he thought how nice a glass of red wine would taste with dinner.

✠

After dinner and the washing up, Graeme sat down in his favourite chair and picked up a novel he had been reading but which had remained sitting idle for the past week and a half. He found it to be a good diversion for a time. The grandfather clock struck ten and Graeme found that he was beginning to nod off. A good night's sleep would probably be in order so that he might be fresh and alert for his meeting with Bishop Halpin in the morning. He was not really looking forward to it. Hours seemed to pass and sleep was not coming to him as his thoughts about tomorrow's meeting swirled in his brain. How was he to approach it? Eventually, sleep came and he fell into a fitful slumber filled with odd dreams.

ELEVEN

Graeme approached the Diocesan Offices just before ten o'clock still uncertain just how he would introduce the conversation. He climbed the stairs to the Bishop's office and approached the secretary in her cubicle. "Good morning," Graeme offered, "I'm Inspector Ingram. I have an appointment with Bishop Halpin this morning."

"Good morning Inspector, I believe he is expecting you. I'll just buzz."

The Bishop's door soon opened and he emerged and welcomed the Inspector.

"Inspector, do come in." The Bishop had a word with the secretary, then came in, and closed the door. He motioned for Inspector Ingram to take one of the two armchairs and then sat in the other one himself. "How are things proceeding, Inspector?" the Bishop asked.

"Well, I received the autopsy and forensic reports yesterday afternoon Bishop and spent the afternoon poring over them to try and fit things together with all of the interviews and enquiries that I've been making."

"And how is it going, then?" asked the Bishop.

Graeme responded, "Well, Bishop, I'm afraid that I've run into a little bit of a conundrum with things, and that is why I wanted to have a chat with you this morning."

"I see," said the Bishop hesitantly. "Is there a problem?"

"I think there is, Bishop, and I don't quite know how to begin this but perhaps I should simply jump in and get to the point."

"That is good, Inspector."

Graeme continued, "Well Bishop, the forensic report indicates that there were two quite fresh drinks glasses in Nigel's room—with scotch residue—both of which had Nigel's and your fingerprints on them."

The Bishop looked at Graeme momentarily with a stunned look on his face, and then said, "Well, Inspector, I told you that my fingerprints might probably be found about the Rectory as I'm a frequent visitor there."

Graeme grimaced inwardly and after a brief but seemingly eternal hesitation, said, "Bishop, I don't quite know how to say this delicately, but the report also found your DNA on Nigel's body..."

Bishop Halpin's eyes widened and his jaw dropped. He appeared to be rendered completely speechless.

And then, total shock set in as the Inspector continued, "...in his anal cavity. I'm so sorry Bishop."

The Bishop turned a brilliant crimson, eyes bulging and then covered his face with his hands and sobbed uncontrollably. Inspector Ingram did not quite know what to do, but offered the Bishop a tissue from a box sitting on the end table. The sobbing seemed to go on forever.

Finally, the Bishop composed himself as best he could, accepted a tissue and wiped his eyes. He then said, "Inspector, I'm so very embarrassed and mortified. I've been living a complete nightmare these past eight or nine days. Actually, I'm relieved because the tension has been unbearable. Let me start from the beginning and try to explain this tragic mess. As you know, I was rector of St. John's before becoming bishop. I had known Nigel since he was a young teenager. As the years passed and I left St. John's I continued to have a connection there as I had become so integrated with the people. Father Justin was kind enough to invite me to say the Friday Mass and to keep my key to the premises. I had always been fond of Nigel and as he matured and became a young adult I discovered that he was also fond of me. We would see each other almost weekly as he was an altar server there and would often serve my Mass. We both felt rather awkward about our friendship and vowed to be extremely discreet about it. I have to tell you that I loved Nigel deeply and he felt the same way. I suppose it was a situation that was bound to end—but I never, ever dreamed that it would end in such a tragic way.

"Bishop, please help me to understand what did happen," Graeme interjected.

The Bishop continued, "Well, on that Sunday evening, Nigel and I were talking on the phone and he explained that Father Justin would be out at a long meeting. I certainly knew of that particular meeting and also that it would indeed be long. Nigel asked me if I might be able to drop over for a while for a drink. I was free that evening and was quite eager to see Nigel, so I accepted. I arrived around 7:30 in the evening, Nigel poured two scotches, and we went up to his room. We sat talking for some time thoroughly enjoying each other's company and the inevitable happened. However, during the course of things I believe Nigel must have had a seizure or heart attack. I remember him telling me about his heart problem some time ago. I was absolutely horrified. I tried desperately to revive him, and some time elapsed. I checked his pulse and found none at all. I knew he had died. I was totally beside myself. Of course, in my panic I was concerned about my own career, about Father Justin and the people of St. John's, but I was also worried for Nigel's sake, and I simply became irrational. I carried him across the hallway to his bathroom, placed him in the tub, and ran water. In my panic I went back to his room and dressed then came back, turned off the water and dropped the hair dryer into the tub so it would appear to be an accident. The lights flashed and the house went into darkness. I then found my way out, got into my car and went home, totally heartbroken and devastated. I think you know what happened after that."

The Bishop again sobbed and cried woefully. Inspector Ingram tried to comfort him and said, "Please, try to pull yourself together, Bishop. This is certainly a very distressing situation and I know you are concerned about the ramifications. "This does place you in a very difficult position, as you are well aware," said the Inspector. "I'm sorry to sound rather blunt Bishop, but you of all people—a pillar of society—must have realized that there would be consequences. Did you not think to call for medical help immediately or to call the police? You must be acquainted with the usual procedures to be applied in such an emergency."

The Bishop seemed dumbstruck for the longest time and continued to sob. Graeme waited, overwhelmed with the awkwardness of the situation. Finally Bishop Halpin spoke. "Inspector, of course I realize now what I probably should have done, and I do feel ashamed and so very heartsick at the whole thing. All I can really say, I suppose, is that I was in an utter panic and reacted irrationally. I was sickened about what happened to Nigel—and of course, I was also concerned about my life and work —literally everything came crashing together like in a bizarre nightmare. At the moment it happened I simply became paralysed. I'm so very ashamed!"

"Bishop," Graeme interjected, "it is all so very tragic, I realize, but what are we to do now?"

"I simply don't know. Things cannot be undone! If only they could be."

"Well, Bishop, I'm going to have to take some time to contemplate all of this and to think about where we go from this point. I suggest that perhaps I should go for now. Could you possibly come to my office at the Yard tomorrow and we can perhaps talk further?"

"Certainly, Inspector. What time would you like me to come—I can move anything that might be scheduled to meet with you."

"Well, perhaps you could come by at about ten in the morning and we can talk again."

"I'll be there at eight then, and I know where your offices are. So dreadfully sorry about all of this, Inspector."

"Alright, Bishop, I'll see you tomorrow."

Bishop Halpin saw the Inspector out after which he spoke with his secretary and cancelled any appointments for the afternoon and evening. He went home and spent a very uncomfortable time thinking and praying. He did not even seem to have any appetite. He thought to himself, over and over, If only this disaster would go away.

TWELVE

Bishop Halpin approached the Scotland Yard building just before ten o'clock and made his way to Inspector Ingram's office. He found that the door was ajar and the lights on. Graeme heard the footfalls in the corridor and rose from his chair to greet the Bishop.

"Good morning, Bishop Halpin. Do come in. I'll hang your coat up here. Please take one of those chairs."

"Thank you Inspector," the Bishop said as he found his way to a seat. "Either one of these, Inspector?"

"Yes, whichever you please. Can I offer you a coffee Bishop?"

"That would be nice, thank you."

Graeme poured two coffees, handed one to the Bishop, indicating the sugar and cream on the corner of the desk and then seated himself.

"Many thanks, Inspector. Well, I had a dreadful

night without much sleep. This has been a totally horrific time."

"It has, of course, disturbed me as well, Bishop. I spent most of last evening just sitting and pondering the situation. Luckily, I was able to get a little sleep, but not that much."

"But I want you to know that I understand your predicament, and as unfortunate as it is, I don't believe that there has been a crime committed. I will therefore conclude my investigation indicating that it was an unfortunate accident and leave it at that."

The Bishop, red eyed and tearful, looked at Inspector Ingram and said, "You can do that?"

Graeme looked back and said, "There is no sense in destroying you, I don't think, and it *was* an accident." The Bishop sobbed even more now and Graeme put his arm around him saying, "Bishop, you take care of yourself, I'll be talking with Father Justin and he will undoubtedly communicate with Nigel's parents and others. No one need know the details but you and me."

The Bishop thanked Graeme tearfully and profusely and was eventually composed sufficiently to leave the office, quietly closing the door behind him.

✠

A Week Later...

A Requiem Mass for Nigel was celebrated at St. John's on Saturday. His parents had driven down from the north country; the parish turned out in great numbers; Justin celebrated the Mass and Bishop Halpin preached a homily, which at Requiem Masses is invariably a matter of saying nice things about the deceased. On this occasion the people probably did not fully comprehend how utterly sincere the Bishop's words were, nor how incredibly difficult it was for him to say them.

After the Mass the people gathered in the Parish Hall to have a glass of wine and to share their fond memories of Nigel. Todd, David and Jason were there along with the Inspector and Nigel's many other friends. Bishop Halpin slipped away quietly after the Mass because he had '*other commitments*' and more than likely realized that he might not be able to control his emotions.

Nigel's body was taken for interment in the churchyard of the village where his parents lived.

"REQUIEM ETERNAM"

PART II

ONE

Justin concluded his evening office in the chapel late on a midweek afternoon, returned to the Clergy House, and settled into his favourite armchair with the mail. He sorted through the day's post to see if there was anything urgent that might need his attention.

It was almost time to begin thinking about putting something together for dinner but his thoughts drifted away as so often happened during this dreadful year. It was almost exactly a year since Nigel's tragic death and Justin wondered, as he had done so often, what he was going to do about his mental state, which was so glaringly deteriorating. Would he never be able to put things to rest and continue with life? He realized with every passing day how much he had relied upon Nigel and how much he missed his amiable company.

He realized he had somehow lost his vitality in parish work and fretted often about what he might do to pull himself together and get back on a productive course. It was beginning to have an effect upon his spiritual life too, and he knew now that the problem was simply not going to vanish of its own accord. He had often thought, in moments when his mind was distracted over the past year, about what he might do to remedy his melancholia. He didn't really have anyone in particular with whom he could pour out his soul. His confessor was a fellow priest in a neighbouring parish but for some reason he didn't feel inclined to open up this matter with him because he knew that it would eventually work its way around to questions about his sexual attractions and within the church community that could be very risky. The Bishop had been sympathetic and encouraging on the few occasions that he had spoken with him, but he realized that no one could really tell him what he should do. One suggestion that Bishop Halpin had made was possibly to talk with Father Kevin about his frame of mind.

Father Kevin was the Prior of Basingshore Abbey, southwest of London on the Sussex coast and the Bishop knew that they had been in seminary together years ago. Both Justin and the Bishop were Benedictine Oblates of the Abbey. He knew that it was a place of reconciliation and strength where there might be some relief and direction for this situation. In addition, Justin and Kevin had been good friends during their seminary years and had been rather candid with each other about personal matters. He knew that this present situation would in all likelihood not surprise Fr. Kevin in the least.

Justin had not actually seen Kevin for several years but thought that a trip to the Abbey might be worthwhile. He just needed someone he felt comfortable with to share his thoughts and this dilemma, which seemed to be so persistent. Heaven only knows, as a priest he was constantly counselling people to unburden themselves and share their deepest concerns rather than allowing them fester. It was truly time he should begin taking his own advice seriously.

Tomorrow he would try to put a call through to the Abbey and see about taking a day or two off to visit and perhaps recharge his batteries. Just the thought of something positive to do about the situation gave Justin the impetus to go to the kitchen and see what he could pull together for dinner. As he had no evening commitments, he decided to pour a whiskey as he prepared his meal.

✠

After Mass and some breakfast the following morning, Justin dealt with correspondence and attended to a few chores that needed doing and soon it was almost ten o'clock. He knew the Abbey routine quite well and thought to himself that this would be a good time to reach someone at the

Abbey's general office. His timing turned out to be exactly right and Father Kevin actually answered the telephone. They chatted for a short while and then began to discuss the possibility of Justin spending a few days there on retreat. It was arranged that he would catch an early train the next morning from Victoria Station and would probably arrive at the Abbey sometime before the noon meal.

The rest of Justin's day was basically tedious and he began to realize how much he was in need of a few days off. Such a pity, he thought, because the daily routine and the customary encounters he had with people had often been such a pleasure for him. It was then that he began to realize he did have a considerable problem. However, he hoped that a few days of retreat and sharing his concerns with Kevin might open the way to regaining his former vitality and zest for life. That was really what was at the root of the situation, he mused, a loss of that zest which had so distinguished his character. It was becoming obvious to Justin that he had never really come to grips with nor understood Nigel's tragic death and furthermore how deeply he had loved him. If his death had simply been accidental then that would be one thing and perhaps easier to deal with, but the nagging question for Justin seemed to be whether or not it might have been suicide—and in that scenario remained the huge question 'but why?' The need to talk to someone and unload all of this mental speculation was critical and he felt a certain sense of relief now that he had called Fr. Kevin and arranged for a few days at Basingshore.

Justin spent part of his evening packing a few necessities in his shoulder bag for the visit to the Abbey and arranging for a colleague to look after mass on the Thursday morning. In a phone call to Bishop Halpin earlier in the day, he explained that he was going to the Abbey for a couple of days and would not be there on Friday for the Bishop's mass. The Bishop offered encouragement to Justin and was pleased to hear that he was taking a few days retreat.

After assembling all the things he would need for the next two days Justin took an early night as the train from Victoria Station the next morning was scheduled to leave at 7:40 a.m.

TWO

It was still quite early when Justin was ready to leave the house and there was ample time so he chose to walk to Victoria Station, the weather being fair. The day was dawning now and the exercise refreshing. In the station he quickly obtained his ticket to Basingshore and found his way to the platform. The train was waiting and he had about eight minutes to find his coach and get comfortably seated. Departure was precisely on the dot and soon the train was wending its way past Wimbledon and Gatwick and on into the neatly ordered Sussex countryside. It was refreshing to be out of the city and soon most of the anxiety that Justin felt had for the moment subsided. The trip would be little more than an hour—a chance to relax and find his bearings. His thoughts were occupied with deciding how he would introduce to Kevin the whole question of why he was feeling so unsettled. He realized that Father Kevin would undoubtedly and intuitively discern what was at the root of his quandary. At any rate he had probably heard through the grapevine about the tragic events of the past year at St. John's. Justin trusted Kevin and decided that he would simply hand over all of his anxiety and let him offer whatever wise advice he might offer. In running this problem over in his mind he was rather pleased that he had thought of speaking with Kevin because he trusted him as a wise and experienced counsellor.

The Sun was now breaking through the cloud cover making patches of green amongst the fences and farm buildings. It seemed the day was insinuating a blessing and Justin's attitude began to brighten with it. This was the slow train, which made an occasional stop here and there on its way to the coast.

Before he knew it, the train was rumbling into the Basingshore station. This was the last stop on this line and the train would begin its journey back to Victoria before very long. Coming out of the station into the High Street, Justin soon hailed a taxi for the four-mile drive to Basingshore Abbey. The day had brightened considerably now and the short drive was pleasant. It felt comforting to be coming back to the Abbey after quite a long time. He could soon make out the Abbey Church and other buildings situated high up on a rise overlooking the Channel. The Abbey church was one of those Victorian, neo-Gothic buildings which emanated a sense of strength and security.

As the cab entered the drive leading to the main entrance to the monk's residence, Justin could see Father Kevin waiting. He had obviously been quite astute as to the timing of the train and taxi.

"Welcome Father", Kevin said as he shook Justin's hand in greeting, "so good to see you again."

"It is good, Kevin. I'm so glad that I was able to come to the Abbey so soon. I'm anxious to begin telling you all about my present dilemma and at least sharing my concerns with you."

"I'm sure you are, Justin, and we will sit down this afternoon and have a good chat. But Noon Day prayers will be in about fifteen minutes, so I think we will get you settled in your room and let you wash up and relax. You are well acquainted with the routine here. I'll meet you outside the church after Noon Day prayers and then we can go to the refectory for lunch."

"Alright," Justin replied with a broad smile, "Will see you then."

He found comfort in settling into the sparse guestroom. Life at the Abbey always radiated such an orderly and reassuring feeling. He emptied his bag, put some things into a drawer and his shaving equipment and toothbrush into the bathroom then rinsed his hands and face. The bell for the Noon Day office began its deep tolling and Justin prepared to go down to the Church. After the office, he found Kevin and they made their way to the Refectory.

The thirty or so monks filed into the refectory

and made their way to their places and Father Kevin led Justin to the head table as was customary when guests visited. There were silent greetings and bows from his friend the Abbot, and when everyone was settled behind their chairs the Abbot led them in the recitation of the Angelus. They then sat and soon a lector announced what was being read during meals at the time and launched into the text. The monks on serving duty that day began to pass around bread, cheese, and bowls of hot vegetable soup. How pleasant it was to be at the Abbey again. This place always gave Justin a spiritual lift. It was so satisfying to feel the sense of community, yet without the noise and clatter that society so often feels is obligatory.

During the meal Justin smiled to himself about the use of sign language, gestures and lip reading involved in passing the condiments, bread and water pitchers. It had truly been a long time since he had visited the Abbey.

When the lector finished his reading, he put the book aside, stepped down from the ambo and sat to eat his meal. When all had finished eating the Abbot jangled his little hand bell, everyone rose, and thanksgiving was returned. The Abbot and head table exited first followed by the rest of the Community. Father Abbot spoke with Justin briefly outside in the hallway and welcomed him to Basingshore. Fr. Kevin asked Justin if he would care to take a short stroll before they went to a quiet room where they could talk privately and catch up on news.

On many occasions Justin had walked around the Abbey Church through these gardens and being there in this special place gave him a marvellous feeling of calm. Kevin remarked on the state of the flowerbeds, which were in their winter phase, and commented that before too long things would need tending to as Spring approached.

Off in the distance, around the other side of the Abbey Church they could hear the shouts and laughter of the seminarians as they engaged in post-lunch recreation before getting back to their classes.

THREE

Entering the main monastic building Father Kevin glanced at his watch as he remarked, "Why don't we meet in the common room in about half an hour? I've one or two things that I must do but then perhaps we can find a quiet corner where we can talk."

"That sounds good Kevin," Justin remarked as he also took note of the time. "I really do appreciate this chance to unload some of the thoughts that have been spinning crazily around in my head these last few months."

"Good. Then we'll meet there in about half an hour. See you then."

Justin felt pleasantly optimistic and buoyed up being in the tranquil atmosphere of the monastery. He picked up the recent copy of the Abbey newsletter and perused the articles including news of the seminary and the Community as he waited until it was time to meet with Fr. Kevin.

✠

The Common Room was two floors below Justin's room. He made his way there at the appointed time and Kevin appeared moments later. They found comfortable lounge chairs in a corner where they could quietly chat. There was only one other monk on the far side of the room near the windows who was engrossed in reading a newspaper.

Once settled in, Father Kevin remarked, "Well, I'm not quite sure when it was I last saw you. I think it must have been about two years ago."

"Yes," Justin replied, furrowing his brow. "I believe you are right. It does seem such a long time, and I'm quite enjoying being here again. Such a place of peace! Which is a welcome change in my present state of mind." He continued without really letting Kevin have a chance to respond, "I suppose you have heard about the tragic events of the past year at St. John's?"

"Yes, indeed I have," Kevin, said quietly, giving Justin a sympathetic half-smile. At first I read about the unfortunate accident in the Guardian, and then some months later I had occasion to talk with Bishop Halpin when he was here on retreat and he was able to explain basically the same information but with a more personal slant, as he had also known the young man. It was certainly a very sad and tragic accident. I want you to know that you have been in our prayers constantly."

"Thank you—I appreciate that. It was indeed sad and tragic," Justin echoed. "The final conclusion was that it was accidental, but I've wrestled for so long now with the possibility that it might have been suicide, that—well, you can imagine why I'm in this rather confused mental state."

"I can only imagine how agonizing that question must be," Kevin replied giving Justin's arm a slight squeeze. "Do you feel like talking about what led up to this horrific event, or would that not be appropriate? I don't mean to intrude."

"No, you're not intruding at all—and I'd be grateful if you would allow me to share it with you. After all, I suppose that is really the reason I've come here. I've not been able to talk to anyone and have simply bottled it up inside myself for the past year—and hence my dilemma."

"Well, I'm happy to listen. Why don't you begin at the beginning and tell me who this young man was. His name was Nigel I seem to recall from the Guardian article."

"Yes, his name was Nigel. Well, I suppose I should begin at the beginning, shouldn't I! When I went to St. John's Nigel was in his early teens. His family was involved in the parish and they lived not far away. So it was a matter of some years that I knew Nigel. Eventually, his parents moved to the north country and Nigel stayed in London as he had a good job. He found an apartment and quite liked

living in the city. He continued to be involved at St.
John's and was an altar server. I grew quite fond of
Nigel to be frank. You are one of the few friends who
ever knew very much about my personal life, so I
suppose that is why I really needed to share all of
this with you. Remember all those times in
seminary years when we talked so candidly about
life and where it was all leading? But, I digress. Let
me pick up my train of thought again. Eventually,
with the downturn in the economy, Nigel was let go
from his job and he could no longer keep his
apartment. He talked with me about his
predicament and although he was searching for
another job, nothing seemed to be working out and
he was thrown into a bit of a panic. We had a few
spare rooms in the rectory and I asked him if he
might consider staying there until something came
into view. He was hesitant, but very thankful and he
moved in about three or four months before this
accident. He was very appreciative and was quite
helpful with cooking, cleaning, and such things. We
also got on very well and it was wonderful to have
the company of someone so concerned and
interested in the parish and in churchy things. We
got on very well."

Father Kevin broke into Justin's narrative briefly
and remarked, "It sounds like you loved Nigel."

"Well, yes, I did!"

"And, if I can ask—did the friendship become
anything more than just a friendship?"

"No, it didn't—it remained a very lovely, Platonic relationship. He was, as he gently put it, attracted to 'older gentlemen'. But, nevertheless, it was wonderful and we had many good times. It was really a relationship of company and support like what you find here in this community."

Kevin again raised a question, "Why are you concerned that his death might have been suicide? Did anything happen that might lead you to think that?"

"No, nothing at all. The only thing that I can suggest is his work situation. But he never made a great issue about the job. In fact he was always quite optimistic about finding another job. He understood that I knew he was constantly searching for work and he realized that there was no pressure on him financially and that he could remain in the rectory for as long as it took. Perhaps that is partly why he was so helpful around the house—and he also knew that I enjoyed his company. It was extremely therapeutic to me to be able to talk with him and discuss the issues of the day and he was extremely intelligent and supportive."

"Did Nigel have many friends," Kevin interjected.

"Well, he had a small group of close friends, not that I knew any of them very well—but he went out with friends fairly often. I had the impression that they might have felt a little awkward being around a rectory and a priest—but whenever they would call they were very courteous on the phone. And I did meet his friend David several times. Nigel was a very sociable young man."

Father Kevin thought for a time in silence and then remarked, "My suggestion would be that you are perhaps placing undue emphasis on this notion of suicide and taking upon yourself unreasonable stress."

"You could be right, I admit, but the solitude of the rectory seems to be conducive to imagining all sorts of things and I can't seem to expunge the idea or get it out of my head."

"I can quite understand my friend."

After another period of silence and contemplation, Father Kevin said, "Listen, Justin, let me do some thinking and praying overnight and tomorrow afternoon let's meet again and continue our talk."

"Certainly—and I do thank you for listening and caring. It has been a long time since I've shared things with anyone other than Nigel."

Kevin responded, "Well, that's what it is all about—and I'm so glad that you decided to come to the Abbey for a few days. You know the routine as to the offices, Mass and meals. I'll see you at mealtimes and perhaps we can meet here tomorrow at about the same time and continue our chat. I have some obligations in the Seminary tomorrow morning but will see you in the afternoon."

"Thank you Father, it is so very good just to

express these anxieties and share them with you."

"That's good. So, I'll see you at dinner time—and try not to fret about things that you can do nothing about!"

✠

Justin spent a good deal of his time in the Abbey Church before the Blessed Sacrament and in his room and in the library reading. The time was well spent and so very beneficial. He thought to himself how good it was to have a break from the life of the parish where his thoughts about the past were constantly reminding him of the happy times he had spent with Nigel. Since Nigel's accident things had just not been the same and as hard as he tried, he could simply not keep himself from dwelling upon this situation. He realized that he was a little out of control and often wondered how he, who was often counselling people with problems, could not deal with his own problems. The proverb alluded to by Jesus, 'physician, heal thyself' seemed to flash into his mind so very often.

The book Justin had chosen to be a framework for his retreat was an analysis of personal worth and discipline written by a psychologist—probably one of those books that the Catholic Church would frown upon—but which was proving to be helpful, none-the-less as he tried to explore how he was coping psychologically with his feelings and self-assessment.

When bedtime came Justin was tired and relaxed. When he awoke in the morning he was surprised at how well he had slept. The country air and quiet was probably part of the reason, but being away from the scene of such anxiety was likely to have contributed to his sound sleep as well.

Justin was looking forward to his meeting again with Father Kevin and to hearing his thoughts about how he might deal with his demons. The morning was pleasant and after breakfast he took a long walk through the countryside, which included a nature walk along the bluffs overlooking the sea. The blustery gusts of wind from the Channel threw his cassock into chaos from time to time but made the hike pleasantly invigorating. He walked at a leisurely pace and tried to time his arrival back at the monastery for noon prayers and lunch. After lunch and some leisurely time in the library it was again time to meet with Father Kevin in the Seminary Common Room.

"Hello again!" Kevin remarked as he entered, "How are you doing today?"

"Much better, thank you. The quiet and atmosphere here have certainly given me a chance to breathe and think. I took a nice long walk this morning along the bluffs and took in some sea air."

"Good," Kevin said reassuringly, "I've certainly been thinking about you a lot since yesterday."

"Thank you. It has been very helpful to be able

to pour things out to you. I'm beginning to feel quite a lot better."

"That's good—and I'm glad you are feeling optimistic. I've given a lot of thought and prayer about this situation and I have an idea that I want to set out to see what you think of it."

"That sounds intriguing!"

"Well, it just might be a solution to a number of situations. Let me begin by telling you about *my* problem—or one of them at any rate. As you know, one of my main functions is heading the Major Seminary. You know Father Basil, I think. For many years he has been teaching New Testament scripture classes. Well, he is getting on in years as you know, and he has felt for some time that he needs to 'retire'—as though a monk could ever retire. But, he has a point, and when the education of new priests is at stake one must take note of the level of teaching. That is not a criticism of Father Basil in any way, but we all need to have a rest. So, as I was ruminating about Basil and you last evening at Chapel, I had a rather creative notion that I thought I might run past you. It could result in killing two birds with one stone—if you can abide that epithet. And I'll put it to you in a question. Would you consider taking on the teaching of those courses? Now, before you answer, you need to have some time to think about it—and I mean weeks or more if necessary. But, I'd just make a few suggestions, which might help the process along. First, you're well qualified for it considering your aptitude for New Testament studies and Greek when we were at the Beda and the Gregorianum in Rome."

Justin's eyebrows arched and his eyes widened considerably hearing this suggestion.

"Now, Justin, before you say anything let me add this. If you were to be interested it would of course be necessary to speak with Bishop Halpin so that, *if* he agrees, he could make arrangements about what to do with St. John's. Also, you would need time to prepare for it, and we would also need to consider the time element—I mean the beginning of semesters and so on. You would of course have rooms here at the Abbey or in the Seminary— whatever would work best. Now, I can tell from your face that this is either a wonderful idea, or perhaps, a shock. I don't know which it is, but do take some time and think about it. Aside from solving some of my problems it would undoubtedly get you out of the scene of that unfortunate accident, which to my way of thinking would surely be better for you. Having talked with the Bishop about your situation, I believe that he would see the sense of this— although, I must assure you that this idea never came up in speaking with him. It miraculously occurred to me just last night!"

They both broke into laughter and Justin said, "Thank you Kevin. This is a complete surprise. I had absolutely no idea what I expected you to suggest or even why I was dumping this whole mess into your lap. It was more that I just needed to talk to somebody about it. I'll go back to London tomorrow much renewed and will think and pray about this."

"Good," Kevin said as he stood and shook Justin's hand. "It could be the beginning of something very good indeed."

"Thank you again. I'll be taking the train back tomorrow morning. This visit has been extremely rejuvenating to say the least, and I'll be contacting you within a fortnight."

FOUR

The taxi came promptly in the morning and within fifteen minutes Justin was at the Basingshore station. Again, the train was ready for boarding and would be departing in five or so minutes—another well timed venture. After leaving the station and clattering through the Basingshore yards they were soon in the midst of the pleasant South Downs. The Sun was shining again and the cheeriness it brought matched Justin's frame of mind. He thought to himself how this trip to the Abbey had likely been a crucial turning point for him. His imagination ran wild for the duration of the trip back to the city; thoughts of a change in venue; questions about getting involved in academic life again and the occasional, if faint, hints of disbelief.

Back in London the sun was shining brightly and the stroll from Victoria Station to the rectory seemed a pleasure—even a welcome back to the city. With so much to consider he hardly knew where to begin, of course, he reassured himself that there was no need to panic. However, he was a little excited and now felt that there just might be a whole new adventure opening up for him. But first things first! Business to attend to and the routine of the parish to step back into. He must begin thinking of all the possible implications as well as to spending a good deal of time in prayer about the future. The very idea did give him goose bumps—in a pleasant sort of way.

✠

Parish work kept up its relentless grind and some extra local neighbourhood council meetings occupied a good deal of Justin's time although he did make room for some reflective time and a lot of prayer about his future. After a week he thought that perhaps it would be appropriate to approach the Bishop for a chat. In the afternoon he picked up the phone, called the Chancery Office, and immediately reached the Bishop's secretary. She was a very pleasant woman and Justin enjoyed talking with her. She was very much aware of the burdens that the clergy often bear and it was good to talk to her. After some relaxed conversation they gradually got around to the purpose of the call. She was able to secure a space of 45 minutes with the Bishop on the Wednesday of the following week. Justin felt that would be enough time to explain his situation and discuss the possibility of responding to the Prior's offer of a teaching post at the seminary. Having made that appointment Justin was able to relax much better feeling that things were finally beginning to fall into place. He could hardly imagine that the Bishop would not be sensitive to his predicament and would be open to cooperating with the plan.

Work was less taxing, it seemed, since he had made the decision to go and talk with Bishop Halpin, and before he knew it Wednesday had arrived. Justin walked to the Chancery Office on yet another sunny and pleasant day. He was a little early for the appointment and enjoyed another friendly chat with the Bishop's secretary, Margaret. She asked Justin how he was doing, fully cognizant of the history of St. John's and the stress that must have resulted for everyone in the parish since the tragic events of the past year. Justin admitted to her that things had been rather troublesome for people and for him especially, and confided that this was actually the reason that he needed to talk with the Bishop. She said that the thought had crossed her mind when this appointment was arranged last week.

Five minutes before the appointed time for Justin's consultation, Bishop Halpin emerged from his office. "Hello Father," he said as he noticed that Justin was already there. "I'm glad you're here early. My telephone calls are all completed now, so please come in. Margaret, I wonder if you might bring us some tea? Would that be good, Father?"

"Yes, Bishop, that would be nice."

They sat down and exchanged pleasantries for several minutes until Margaret entered with a tray of tea and biscuits, then made her exit. She remarked just before she closed the door, "I'll take messages Bishop, so as not to disturb your conversation."

"Thank you, Margaret."

Taking their seats again, with tea and biscuits within easy reach from the coffee table, Bishop Halpin remarked, "Well, Father, how have you been lately? It's been quite a while since we talked, hasn't it."

"Well, Bishop," Justin said, "things haven't really been that good for me personally. That is really why I wanted to talk to you. I suppose that I've not been able to deal with Nigel's death very well. I simply can't seem to accept that his death was accidental and my mind seems to be determined not to let go of the idea that it might have been suicide. I continually rack my brain to try and imagine what might have made him do such a thing. Of course, as it happened in the rectory, I'm reminded of him constantly. Everywhere I look or go I'm reminded of the rather happy times that were a part of sharing conversations and meals in the rectory. Even in church I think about it because, as you know, he was so involved with everything in the parish.

"Father, I can imagine the stress you must be

under. However, I understand how the idea of suicide must be very repugnant to you. It has the same effect on me, and I feel certain that he did not take his own life. However, I realize that it is not so easy to simply shut down your thoughts."

"No, Bishop, it certainly is not easy. And I think that I really do need a change of venue. That is actually the reason I've come here today. I went to Basingshore Abbey recently for a little retreat, as you know, and during my stay I had an opportunity to talk with Father Kevin about all of this. Before leaving the Abbey we chatted for a second time and he came up with a rather interesting suggestion.

The seminary is going to need someone to replace Father Basil who, as you know, has taught New Testament scripture and some other related classes for many years. He is well into his eighties and the poor man deserves a rest. Father Kevin suggested that I might take on that work and that it would give me the change of venue that I need, as well as a new focus that might be in order considering the circumstances. Of course, talking with you about this idea is germane to everything."

"I see," the Bishop said with a concerned tone of voice. "Well, Father, I must be honest with you and do a little explaining myself. As you know, I've been aware of your situation—acutely aware to be more precise—and I have to confess that I've shared my concern about you with Father Kevin. So he realizes that I understand and that I'd do anything in my power to assist in resolving your plight."

Justin's face brightened realizing that there had been such collaborative concern, and he remarked, "I'm glad that you were able to talk with Father Kevin about all of this—very glad indeed."

The Bishop continued, "Father, I completely agree that you do need a change." His brow wrinkled for a moment as he pondered silently. Justin waited expectantly. Finally, the Bishop looked at Justin with great compassion in his eyes and began very slowly, "Father, I think this idea of teaching is excellent, and you are undoubtedly very well qualified for it. Also, the change of venue, as you remarked, would be just what you need—and I can't think of a better change than to be at the Abbey. What I suggest is that I arrange for another priest to take your position at St. John's—say in a few months—and you can begin to deal with the seminary and Father Kevin. That will obviously take some time as well. These things don't just happen over night as you well know."

Justin beamed, "Thank you so much Bishop. I can't tell you what a relief this news is to me. I'll contact Father Kevin and we will see where it goes from there. I'm sure he will also be in touch with you."

"Father, I'm sure this will sort itself out now and that it will bring a sense of closure to you. The change will also be hugely beneficial to you and to the Abbey, I'm sure," the Bishop remarked.

Before Justin left the Bishop's office he asked

the Bishop's blessing and knelt down. He was enormously grateful that the Bishop understood and that he was happy to cooperate with this plan.

✠

Sleep overcame Justin deeply that evening. Unlike so many nights during the past year he was able to rest completely without the unpleasant dreams and restlessness. Simply knowing that there would be a new direction in his life was liberating. His obsession with Nigel's death might now be put to rest finally and he could get on with things. He awoke at 6:00 a.m. as usual, but he felt fresh and eager to get into the day. Once the morning obligations were attended to he would try to contact Father Kevin and give him the happy news of his meeting with the Bishop.

The first attempt at mid-morning was not successful. Fr. Kevin was not available but it was suggested that he try again at around eleven thirty. Busying himself with correspondence and telephone calls, Justin passed the morning and soon it was time to make another attempt to call. Fr. Kevin must have been informed about the earlier call, as he was in the office and answered on the second ring. Justin recounted a brief version of what happened the day before and Father Kevin was nodding his head in agreement as he listened. He even admitted that he had discussed the issue with the Bishop on several occasions. Justin laughed about his admission and said that the Bishop had also indicated that he had spoken to Kevin about the situation. The next step, Father Kevin suggested enthusiastically, would be for Justin to come back to the Abbey for perhaps another two day visit so that they could do some planning about timing and to sit down with Father Basil in order to discuss academic questions which would then allow Justin to make the transition into the life of the Seminary. Justin explained that the Bishop had asked that he continue at St. John's for at least a few months until he could arrange for another priest to take his place. After consulting their agendas they came to a decision about when would be the best time for another visit to the Abbey and they inked it in. Justin was happy to feel that things were moving along this quickly. There was now some light at the end of the tunnel.

After this most productive telephone call Justin went about the rest of the day with an uplifted heart. Expectation about this rather considerable change in his work enabled him to go about the present daily routine with a sense of confidence. Bishop Halpin had suggested that he would want to spend a Sunday at St. John's soon to speak to the parish about Justin's move and to announce the identity of the new priest. But this would take place sometime in the next few weeks when a replacement had been negotiated. The people of the parish, of course, were quite cognizant of the stresses and associations that the events of the past year had placed upon Justin. They would in all probability understand and be prepared to send off their beloved priest with their support and affection.

The next visit to Basingshore Abbey came rather quickly Justin thought. Surprising how time passes when one is relaxed and has a goal in sight. The appointed day came and off he went to Victoria Station. The trip seemed shorter this time and soon he was met at the Basingshore station by Father Kevin with an Abbey vehicle. Their conversation on the ride to the Abbey was affable as they began to consider how Justin's life would soon unfold in the context of this new chapter.

FIVE

After settling into a room in the Seminary building it was almost time to go to the Abbey Church for the noonday office and then lunch. As he knelt in the silence he thanked God for this new adventure and for the welcome and sense of family that was rekindled in this Benedictine atmosphere. The simple life rooted in Benedict's rule is framed by the tenet *Ora et Labora;* Pray and Work. The Benedictines had never allowed their spirituality to become consumed with extreme penance or depravation but had retained a healthy sense of hospitality and enjoying from time to time the bounty of Creation—regarding good food and drink as God's gift—always aware of the joy of God's bounty. Justin revelled in the serenity and quiet, infused with the sweet smell of the incense lingering from the morning's mass mingled with the odour of the oil from the sanctuary lamps.

Monks and seminarians gradually drifted in and

took their places in choir with almost no sound, quietly reverencing the altar and the Blessed Sacrament as they did so. The bell pealed the hour and Abbot Placidus and the gathered assembly stood and began to chant the office. Justin's heart soared and he intuitively felt that he would find this new phase of his life to be exciting and challenging.

At lunch the lector read from the Rule of Benedict and the section he read seemed ironically apt to Justin. It was from Chapter 60 of the Rule and dealt with the question of priests who might wish to live in the monastery. It specifies that such a priest should accept and live by the Rule and stability and that he may, with the permission of the Abbot, give blessings and celebrate Mass. He received this reading in a very personal way in spite of the fact that the lector was simply going through the Rule in sequence meal by meal.

After lunch there was going to be a meeting with Father Kevin and Father Basil to deal with some of the matters pertaining to the New Testament courses he would be teaching. It would naturally be important to make a smooth transition and to pick up where Father Basil leaves off.

A brief rest period followed lunch after which the three of them met in a classroom—Father Basil appearing with a huge stack of binders and notes.

"Well, Fathers," Kevin began, "no need for introductions as we've known each other for some years."

Father Basil took Justin's hand and shook it warmly, "I'm so glad, Father, that you've decided to accept this position. As you know I've been teaching here for decades and it is about time that I retired from the classroom. I'm entirely confident that you will pick up the thread and be a valuable member of the Seminary staff."

"Thank you Father—I'm honoured to be following you and joining the Seminary staff and living within this Community."

Kevin repeated Father Basil's welcome and gave him leave to take charge of this introductory meeting.

"We have both had some quite lengthy discussions about your joining us Father, and perhaps I can cover some of the main thoughts that we have entertained. Firstly, we will be coming up to the end of this semester in several months—it would be an appropriate time for you to begin when the new semester begins. I realize that you will be at St. John's for a couple of months until the Bishop appoints a new priest there. But, when you have finished and made your move to the Abbey, perhaps you would like to spend a few weeks sitting in on classes to get a feel for what we have done in the past and also to get to know the seminarians a little. That will also work well in letting them become acquainted with you. I've brought a number of books and sets of notes so that you can see what and how we have proceeded in the past. I realize that every teacher has his own personal style and I'm not suggesting at all that you copy the way I've gone about it. However, among these documents are reading lists and course outlines which I'm sure you will find standard and of assistance. There are also outlines for papers and examinations from over the years, which might be of interest to you. You will also see that with respect to the Pauline corpus, and the other epistles, they have been introduced by date of writing and by author—at least as much as we can ascertain. Sometimes they are associated by their content as well. Similarly, there are notes and class work papers and exams for the Greek course, which I've also taught. And there are numbers of copies on hand of *Machen's, New Testament Greek for Beginners*—probably the best book currently available on the subject—as well as copies of other text books related to scripture studies. I've also divided the materials up with respect to the three-year programme of the Major Seminary."

During the course of their meeting Justin had a number of queries, on which Father Basil was able to shed light. It was apparent that both the Prior and Father Basil were pleased with Justin's eagerness and his questions. It was quite obvious that he would adjust quickly to this new adventure. He too was pleased with this opportunity and was eagerly looking forward in anticipation to life at Basingshore.

When the meeting was concluded Kevin

reminded Justin that Abbot Placidus would like to meet with him later that evening to welcome him to the Community and to offer some suggestions about his move to the Abbey.

✠

After dinner that evening the Abbot approached Justin in the hallway, took his arm, and walked with him to a corner of the monk's common room where they could sit and chat. Abbot Placidus was a robust man in his mid fifties with a gentle nature and bushy eyebrows. Although he was a mitred Abbot, in his normal habit he was indistinguishable from the other monks save for his pectoral cross pendent on its gold chain. Justin marvelled at how ordinary he appeared and how humble, at the same time knowing full well that an abbot is in a sense equal in rank to a diocesan bishop and that the Community he leads is really an independent entity. This arrangement is integral to the Benedictine way and has for many centuries enabled them to offer objective instruction and teaching—especially in their oversight of seminaries.

Once they were comfortably seated the Abbot began, "Father Kevin tells me that you had a very good meeting with Father Basil about the courses he has been teaching here for such a long time. And also that Basil is pleased with your interest and background. I'm sure that you will readily fit into our life here at Basingshore."

"Thank you, Father Abbot. And I'm equally as excited about the prospects."

"I understand that at some point, when you are free from St. John's, you will move here and be able to sit in on some of Fr. Basil's lectures and get to meet our seminarians. There is a two-room suite in the seminary building that I think you might find quite comfortable. It will probably be much more suitable than a cell in the monastery, and I've already spoken to Fr. Kevin about it. He quite agreed with the idea".

"That sounds rather intriguing, Father Abbot. Thank you so much."

"You will be able to take meals either in the seminary refectory during term where meals are not silent, or in the monastic refectory, whenever you choose. Perhaps you might like to alternate on occasion. Sharing meals with the seminarians and interacting with them will be extremely worthwhile. It is one of the things I wish I had been able to do more often."

"That sounds a good idea" Justin interjected.

Father Placidus continued, "I've thought a good deal about your taking this position as technically not a member of the Community, but as you are an oblate of the order, I think that perhaps it would be appropriate for you to assume our habit and consider yourself to be under the same rule as the rest of us—in truth you are anyway. I'll have Father

Swithun prepare a scapular and cowl for you to wear with your cassock.

"I'll be most honoured, Father."

"If you have any questions during the coming months before you move here, you can address them to Father Kevin and I'm certain we can work out any details. I look forward to your joining us Father."

They parted with a handshake and Justin joined Father Kevin who was sitting in a far corner of the common room reading. He recounted his visit with Father Abbot and expressed his contentment with the way things were unfolding.

When he retired that evening he mused on the events of the day and fell into a pleasant slumber knowing that things were falling into place—a calm that he had not often experienced during the past year.

SIX

The routine of parish life continued now with a new focus, which enabled Justin to put aside his former worries and the nagging thoughts that had plagued him for almost a whole year. His vision was now toward the future and much less on dwelling so frequently about the past. His whole attitude had struck a new course and been reshaped. Dealing with the daily chores of parish life seemed much less irksome than they had come to be and his encounters with people took on a brighter tone. He wondered if parishioners had noticed his morose attitude even though he had tried to disguise his inner feelings. Comments of late seemed to indicate that people had noticed his new stance on things.

Bishop Halpin contacted Justin within a few weeks and told him that he had things in hand and that the appointment of a new priest would be made soon. He suggested that now might be a good time for Justin to make it known so that the people would have ample time to digest the news. It would also be appropriate to let the parish know that he would be accepting the teaching post at the Seminary.

Justin worked all afternoon that day on his resignation announcement trying to discreetly explain his desire to move into the teaching position and yet his sadness in leaving St. John's and the people he had come to love so dearly. He was able to refrain from mentioning Nigel's accident knowing that it was common knowledge in the parish that he had suffered a significant depression, which in essence had been caused by the unfortunate incident.

After Justin's announcement at Mass the next Sunday most people were supportive realizing that he needed a change of direction, although a few found it a little disappointing as they had become rather fond of their priest. But, even they were happy for him as they realized how pleased he seemed to be about the move. With the time frame now determined it would be natural for St. John's to begin preparing for Father's going away—and perhaps a celebratory banquet on the Sunday preceding his departure. The new priest apparently would be able to spend a few days with Justin so that certain details and practical information could be passed on.

A telephone call to the Abbey and a chat with Father Kevin produced the plan for another visit to begin planning more concrete details about his move as well as to spend more time with Fr. Basil in preparation for taking on his teaching regimen. It had also been decided that Justin would spend some weeks sitting in on Father's classes to gain a clear understanding of where things were moving and to get a feel for Father Basil's approach as well as seeing how the Seminarians interacted with their teachers.

He was becoming ever more and more excited about this new venture and had begun to do reading and note taking on the subject matter that he would be discussing in class.

✠

Several weeks passed before Justin's next visit to Basingshore and he had begun to sort through his books and belongings in preparation for the day when he would make the move. In his typical way, he made lists of things he would need to take and placed them in a particular corner of his rooms. He mused on how little there would actually be to transport as he lived a rather frugal and simple life as far as material things were concerned. Several items he would want to take were put in a valise, which he would take on this next visit. Each time he took the train to Basingshore he became a little bit more excited about his move.

Arriving at the Abbey, Justin was welcomed as usual, but he sensed a certain feeling of family now that it was known by everyone what was actually unfolding. Father Basil was particularly warm and convivial and it crossed Justin's mind that he must indeed be looking forward to handing over his duties and beginning his retirement. And it occurred to him that having Father Basil so handy he would be able to share concerns with him at almost any time, which gave him an added sense of confidence.

During this visit he explored the rooms that would be his home after the move. They were in the Seminary block and were two adjoining rooms—a sitting room and a small bedroom with a bathroom—undoubtedly meant to be the quarters for a principal. As Father Kevin was the Principal, his quarters were his cell in the Monastic complex.

When Justin entered his new rooms he saw that the promised scapular and cowl had been laid out on the bed. They seemed to symbolize the silent assurance of his place within the Community.

It was enormously comforting to feel that this Community would be his family soon. Although he was completely familiar with the routine of the Abbey—having visited so many times in the past—he felt now that he would be more than a visitor, but a family member. He loved the quiet of the place: the tranquil and ordered worship in the Abbey Church, the contemplative meals and the friendship of fellow priests and brothers. Of course he also looked forward to the interaction with the students in the Seminary and the discussions that would be an integral part of the academic work. He had so enjoyed his own seminary years and looked forward with anticipation to that invigorating atmosphere.

✠

The day of the farewell celebration for Justin finally arrived. Several of his priest friends had come along so that they could have a proper festive High Mass on that Sunday evening which would then be followed by a gala banquet. Parishioners had been busy for several days in the kitchen of the parish hall preparing delicacies, arranging tables and decorating the hall.

More members than usual had appeared to form a choir and the music was suitably chosen to include some of Justin's favourites—including the setting for the Mass. Justin was having mixed emotions throughout the proceedings—a bit of sadness at his leaving but a good deal of delight at the overwhelming turnout of people from the parish and personal friends. His thoughts wandered through time from the days when Nigel was staying at the rectory to the excitement of taking up his new position at the Abbey.

Much goodwill and appreciation for Justin's time at St. John's was expressed by those who spoke and he responded noting many of the happy memories of his time there as well as his eagerness to take on the new work of teaching.

After the evening was officially over, people

lingered and talked for what seemed hours as though they might will it not to conclude. Eventually, with the clean up done and the last of the guests departing, Justin went back to the rectory with his two clerical friends to imbibe in a scotch and relax after what had been an entirely delightful evening.

About midnight his two colleagues collected their coats and wishing Justin well, took their leave, stepping out into the dark winter night. As he waited for sleep to come he mused on the events of the evening and felt a sense of security and liberation—a feeling that he had not enjoyed for such a long time. Sleep soon came and Justin rested soundly throughout the night.

SEVEN

Father Reginald who would replace Justin arrived at the Clergy House door four days before Justin was to set off for the Abbey. He was known to Justin through his work on diocesan committees and he thought to himself what a wise decision the Bishop had made. The parish, which he had loved so much, would be in capable hands. They moved Fr. Reginald's belongings into the guest room for the time—the room that had been Nigel's. He would, after Justin's departure, be able to move into the larger suite of rooms, which Justin had enjoyed for all those years. It was fortunate that they would have these few days together to talk about some of the important issues involving the parish and to exchange thoughts about directions and ongoing projects. Justin was able to create a list of key people who would be able to assist the new pastor as well as some notes. Of course, it wasn't that Justin would be that far away in case of urgency—a telephone call or an email, if necessary, would in all likelihood resolve any questions.

Over the course of their time working together Justin became increasingly assured that this was going to work out remarkably well. Father Reginald's style was relaxed and personable and Justin could see that he would be well received by the people of the parish. He was even able to share with Reginald the sad experience that had happened a year ago and how he had become obsessed with trying to understand what had really happened. Father Reginald had heard about the incident as one does, within a community like the Diocese, and he revealed that he too had wondered about the circumstances, but he encouraged Justin to accept the decision of Scotland Yard—that it had been an accident—to put the incident from his mind and get on with this new venture.

Finally, the day of Justin's departure for the Abbey arrived and Reginald helped to move the relatively small amount of luggage to the front door. He had already sent on some boxes of books and other personal belongings to the Abbey, in addition to items he had transported on his various visits, so that today's trip would be a little easier. Dr. Landsworth and several others from the parish came by to wish Justin well and to see him off. As the cab moved off into the afternoon traffic Justin waved to them through the back window and they were doubtless unaware of the glint of tears.

✠

The now familiar train journey was uneventful. It was a pleasant afternoon and the tranquil countryside seemed to give Justin a palpable sense of detachment from the past. Thoughts of this new venture occupied his mind as the train sped on toward the coast and his expectations began to occupy his mind more and more. The future began to look bright and he was pleased that things had evolved as they had. Arrangements were made with the Abbey about his arrival today and one of the monks would be there at the station with a vehicle to transport him and his luggage to the monastery.

The young monk who appeared at the station quickly loaded the luggage and a cardboard box containing books and assorted documents into the car. They would arrive at the Abbey in plenty of time to settle in and prepare for Vespers and dinner. Someone had been busy in Justin's rooms arranging the things that had already arrived which gave him a most welcoming and pleasant feeling. He smiled to himself as he glanced at the cowl still neatly in place on the bed. Once he had washed his face and arranged a few of the things he'd brought he put on his cassock and the new scapular and prepared to go to the Abbey Church for Vespers.

After the Office the Abbot and Father Kevin caught up with Justin and welcomed him. They apologized for not having reached him before Vespers so that he could be shown to the place in choir, which he would occupy. But, they assured him that his place in the monk's refectory would be pointed out. Now that he was no longer a guest he would take his place—according to his dignity at the appropriate refectory table rather than at the head table. He was now beginning to feel entirely like he belonged and it gave him an overwhelming sense of peace.

It was Friday, which means that Justin would have a chance to relax and spend the weekend attending to his devotions and establishing himself at the Abbey before classes resumed on Monday. He was rather looking forward to those classes—seeing Father Basil in action—and in meeting the students formally. He would be observing for several weeks and for this he had a notepad ready to jot down any information and queries, which would be crucial to his taking Father Basil's place. At the Conventual Mass on Sunday he was able to discern that there were more seminarians than he had realized, assuming that most of them were together in their place in the church. Of course, he realized that their numbers represented all three years of the theology programme. The Mass was beautiful, dignified and simple, the smoke of the incense swirling in shafts of sunlight from the clerestory windows and the haunting Gregorian chant filling the church with a sense of serenity. Father Abbot preached a very carefully conceived but brief homily, and Justin thought to himself how it spoke to the highly disciplined and circumspect atmosphere of the Abbey and of the Benedictine life.

The Benedictines had always striven to follow a style of life that was rooted in prayer and work with an appreciation for the good things of life principally in the areas of hospitality, and food and drink. The drink aspect—wine in particular—had undoubtedly been an important aspect of Benedict's Rule because of the difficulties in procuring potable water in his time, but it is also a tangible expression of thanksgiving for God's bounty and of fellowship with the Creator. The Community gathers at various times throughout the day for the singing of the daily offices and mass, which form the structure of the day. Interspersed in that regimen are a multitude of other tasks which all contribute to the life of the monastery and in which all the brethren who are physically able share in. Work involving the monastery vegetable and herb gardens and grounds keeping; the tending of cattle; bee keeping; cooking and cleaning are all aspects of the work of the household. The teaching that Justin would be engaged in is also part of the monastic structure, but as a member of the Community Justin would also take his place in the roster of monks who serve at table in the refectory and who read during the silent meals.

EIGHT

When lectures resumed on Monday morning Justin went with Father Basil after breakfast to the classroom where the third year group of New Testament students would meet. The room with its podium at one end had long table-desks along the sides and back in a 'U' shape. The sounds of seminarians could be heard from the distant recesses of the long hallway, chattering and laughing, Justin had found his way to a place at back of the room, and chosen a seat. Within minutes seminarians began to drift in and take their places. Several of them had met Father Justin already on visits to the Abbey and they nodded courteously to him knowing of the change that would soon be taking place. When all had settled in and were accounted for, Father Basil moved to the podium and began with the usual invocation that opened their studies.

"Fratres, Good morning. I'm sure you have seen

Father Justin from time to time over the past few months when he was visiting and know that he will be taking my place teaching New Testament studies. Let me formally introduce Father Justin who is sitting at the back of the classroom. Welcome Father —we are very happy to have you with us."

Justin stood momentarily and thanked Father Basil for his welcome.

Father continued, "Father Justin, as I'm sure you know, is well qualified for this task, having done splendid work in scripture studies and Greek at the Beda and the Gregorianum in Rome. He will be sitting in from time to time as this semester plays out and will commence teaching my courses when I retire at the end of this semester. I will still be around of course, but will rejoice in passing on the burden of teaching to Father Justin. You will have plenty of opportunity to introduce yourselves to him and talk with him as he will occupy a suite of rooms in the Seminary Block and will be taking meals in the seminary refectory. When he needs to get away from you and have some quiet he will join us for certain meals in the monk's refectory."

"Now, in our last session we were nearing the end of Paul's Letter to the Romans—chapter 15— where he admonishes the community about the importance of the written word to infuse in the church a sense of comfort and hope."

He continued with his teaching and Justin busied himself with noting his approach and in making notes to himself.

✠

Over the period of the week Justin sat in on all of Father Basil's classes and was introduced to the members of each of the three years of seminarians as well as to have a glimpse of what each of the classes was engaged in studying. Because these courses in New Testament studies are only one of about eight disciplines that make up the curriculum, it involved about twelve hours during the span of a week. Seminarians also had classes in liturgics, church history, canon law, homiletics and sermon preparation, Old Testament studies, and study of the Church Fathers. The course load was indeed intense and was a full time occupation for the students, who needed as well, time for recreation and leisure. A soccer field adjoined the Seminary Block and on occasion Justin was encouraged by the seminarians to join them, which he was happy to do.

In addition to Justin's sitting in on classes during that month there was also opportunity to sit down with Father Basil to go over the profiles of most of the seminarians so that he had some idea of their background and special needs, but Father Basil reminded him often that as he got to know them these things would make themselves known, even as he himself came to understand his students. Basil remarked several times how much he would miss the close contact with them, but was happy that he would not be far away, and would be able to remain in touch with them, at least until they had completed their studies and moved on. Father Basil knew that a certain number of them might find that they had vocations to remain with the Community, and that thought always gave him a certain delight.

One of the seminarians that Basil commented upon was a first year student named Marc Sinclair, who he explained had come by way of the Anglican Church. He remarked with a rather cryptic smile and after a short space of private thought, "You know, Marc is a very bright young fellow and I've found him to be eager to engage in discussion. He often asks quite insightful questions, and he certainly has done considerable reading. I understand his eagerness, but something inside me says that his transition to the Catholic Church just might be fraught with a certain sort of—what shall I say—difficulty. I mean it is quite a step. I don't wish to sound sceptical, Father, but I'm just, well, curious. He made this step a number of years ago when he was about nineteen. I believe he is now twenty-six."

Father Basil's musing seemed to trail off a bit as he thought about Marc, and Justin waited a little before interjecting, "Yes, I understand what you are saying, Father. He came and sat at my table during dinner the other night and was quite an interesting conversationalist. He seemed to be taking it upon himself to welcome me on behalf of the seminarians.

During our discussion he did inform me, very briefly, a bit of his background and I found him to be extremely pleasant." Justin's thoughts wandered to that dinnertime discussion and he reminisced about how he had thought Marc was so very like Nigel in his manner and outgoing personality. He was also quite like Nigel in his height and proportions with dark hair and a somewhat Mediterranean look with the shadow of heavy facial hair and penetrating eyes. Justin found him to be quite alluring—but he also thought that he ought to put that notion completely out of his mind.

✠

During the ensuing two months Justin continued to be involved with the Seminary, both in sitting in on classes and in making his preparation of class materials and lecture notes. Marc was frequently a mealtime conversationalist as were several of the other seminarians. There were times when Justin and Marc would go for walks after dinner in the Abbey grounds and Justin found that he was becoming quite fond of Marc. The evenings were at this time getting longer and the weather quite pleasant—after all it was nearing the end of the spring semester. Soon the seminarians would be going to work for the summer months in various parish situations where they would gain experience in the day-to-day affairs of their priestly calling.

Marc would be going to work in a London parish where the Rector was a friend of Justin's. He was able to give Marc a little knowledge about the parish and priest and Marc seemed to be pleased with the prospect. He was anticipating the experience. He asked Justin if he might write to him over the course of the two and a half month summer break. Justin was happy to keep in touch—in fact he was overjoyed. He would be spending those months deep in study and preparation for the beginning of the new academic year in September.

Before the end of May a series of ordinations occurred when some seminarians of the third year of theology were either made deacons or were ordered to the priesthood. One of these was a fellow who was already in deacon's orders and who would be joining the Benedictines. His ordination to the priesthood took place in the Abbey Church and the local Bishop of that Sussex diocese presided. It was timely that it took place before the students dispersed for the summer because they were all able to be present. Justin was able to attend two other ordinations, which were both in London parishes. He travelled into the city with Marc by train as he was on his way to his summer placement. This made the hour and a quarter journey most pleasant as Marc was never without interesting things to talk about. They said their goodbyes after the first of the ordinations when Marc was driven to his summer quarters in the parish he had been assigned to. On leaving he repeated his promise to write, and Justin was quietly warmed.

Justin stayed in the city for two nights and then after the second ordination he returned to the Abbey. The journey to Basingshore was this time very quiet. He thought about Marc and realized that he was going to miss him over these next few months.

NINE

Summer at the Abbey was very pleasant and Justin had ample time and solitude in which to do his preparations and work on lesson plans. He took his meals in the Monk's Refectory during July and August and for that time was content to fall in with the routine of the Abbey taking his turn at serving table.

As promised, a letter from Marc arrived sometime during that first few weeks of the summer break and Justin was secretly delighted. He took the letter to his rooms after the noonday meal and enthusiastically opened it. Marc was enjoying his involvement in the parish. He went on in some detail describing his routine and chatted on about many things as he routinely did in conversations. He spoke of his work with parish groups and described his accommodation in the rectory and the church. He was quite happy with everything it seemed, although he did say that he had missed their conversations during meals and their walks in the Abbey grounds. He ended his letter with the salutation, "Agaph, Marc".

Well, thought Justin, he certainly has been paying attention in his Greek classes. "Love" seemed a little straightforward—however, he lectured to himself that in English we only have one word for this whereas in Greek there are several with nuanced connotations. Surely he meant it as in the phrase, *'see how the Christians love one another'*. Justin blushed a little inwardly but was in truth overwhelmed.

During the course of the next two months Justin poured himself into his preparation work and there were countless times when he met with Father Basil to discuss details and ask for his thoughts. It seemed that Father Basil was truly happy to finally be retired from the Seminary work, but that he enjoyed their chats and, of course, the opportunity to offer advice. His heart was very much with the many students he had nurtured over the decades.

✠

During the first part of the summer break Justin devoted his time to his introductory lectures for the new group of first year seminarians. He remembered from his own experience of beginning in seminary how he had made the assumption that the Sacred Scriptures are simply there in black and white and that it would simply be a matter of learning what was contained in them. What young, would-be Priest wouldn't think that? But, to his dismay, he discovered that it was not all that simple. He was soon to learn that there were many issues to be addressed before even getting at how the Church interprets Holy Scripture.

Justin thumbed through Father Basil's course outlines and other materials before even beginning to formulate his own lecture notes. He was now, of course, quite aware that within the Church there were many different positions taken with regard to how one approaches scripture. How often had he heard Catholics expressing great surprise that there was not just one, simple Catholic position on matters of doctrine coming from scripture. And further, that people are surprised to discover that a good deal of teaching is rooted more in the Magisterium than in Sacred Scripture. As he began formulating his thoughts on this he was rather glad that he was going to be teaching scripture rather than dealing with dogma and the Magisterium.

In consulting Father Basil's notes Justin was pleased to see that he took a more open approach to the question of the authority of scripture. He found references about early palimpsests, vellums and parchments; about Marcion and his concerns about the Old Testament and the canon; about Tatian, Origen and Eusebius and their unease with respect to texts; continuing up to the nineteenth century theological discourses on scripture. It didn't really surprise him very much, as this was probably the case in most Benedictine Houses. It became obvious to him that Basil had dealt with the whole range of questions about biblical content, from the earliest centuries and on up to the relatively recent developments of the nineteenth century, including the textual criticism and new thinking of the German Schools of theology. Justin grinned to himself when he read over notes, which dealt with the University of Tübingen's involvement in the question of biblical criticism.

All of this information was to Justin a great relief—he would be able to go ahead and teach the subject in its fullness without worrying about anyone from within the hierarchy objecting to his thorough and informed approach to New Testament studies. In addition the seminarians would be using the Jerome Biblical Commentary as a resource text, which contained the work of a host of eminent and celebrated theologians.

During these months of preparation to teach Justin met quite frequently with Father Basil to discuss details and to glean new ideas for his courses. He was eager to continue the good work that Father Basil had done yet he wished to inject some vigour and current thinking so that new crops of men would be prepared to go out into the workaday world equipped to meet the challenges of parish life.

Marc's letters continued to arrive throughout

that summer and Justin was intrigued to reply and continue the friendship that was developing. He felt that a great void had been filled in his personal life, which complimented and sustained his new endeavour in teaching.

✠

Summer break was almost over now as the last week in August came. Gradually the sounds of cheerful conversations in the Seminary hallways began again. Classes would begin early in September and Justin was eager to begin his teaching in earnest. Marc came back a few days before classes began and he made a point of finding Justin in the refectory at lunch time on the day he carried his luggage to his room. They were both quietly happy to see each other again and Marc asked if they might take a walk that evening along the country road that led to the monastery in order to catch up on news and discuss things that they would not have wanted to write in letters. After dinner they took the opportunity to do so before Compline after which the Great Silence would begin.

Marc chatted away eagerly telling Justin all about his involvement in the parish and about the Rector—he seemed to have a huge store of anecdotal material to share. Justin was quiet for most of the walk simply delighting in Marc's enthusiasm and having him back again. When asked how his summer had gone Justin took a little time explaining his research and reading as well as his meetings with Father Basil. He expressed how glad he was that Father Basil seemed to be happy with his approach, and how he was looking forward to the term beginning. He had already met a few of the new, first year seminarians who were arriving day by day. Father Kevin was kept busy with receiving the new students, assigning them to rooms and explaining the rules and expectations of the Seminary and the Community.

TEN

Late on Sunday evening Justin did some familiarization of his preparation work. He began to think that, at least at the beginning, he was going to feel a sense of pressure, until he got used to the pattern. He began by trying to memorize the teaching schedule as it pertained to the scripture courses and then to distinguish just which years would be doing the various portions of the New Testament. The new First Year seminarians would have a class on the Monday morning and would spend a little time introducing themselves and be given an introductory survey of the years work, which would consist of a survey of the historical evolution of the origins of texts; some reference to the canon of Scripture, and notes about the four Gospels.

The Second Year students, which would be Marc's class, would be spending the year studying the Acts of the Apostles, and a certain number of St.

Paul's Epistles.

The Third Year students would be spending most of their time working with the Catholic Epistles; those of Peter, James, Jude and John as well as the Apocalypse of John.

Each of the years would have two classes each week in New Testament studies in addition to all their other courses except when special Feast Days pre-empted the study regimen. It would be quite a gruelling schedule indeed—for both Justin and the seminarians.

✠

On Monday morning the new First Year students arrived in the appointed classroom and took seats before Justin arrived with his attaché case and settled himself at the lectern. He looked around, did a mental count, and determined that there were fifteen of them.

When all were settled and silence prevailed, Justin began. "Good Morning Gentlemen. I'm Father Justin. I presume you have all managed to find your way around the Abbey Church, the Seminary building and the grounds and have become comfortable in your rooms. I believe we have all met at meals, at recreation time and especially at the wine and cheese evening last night. As you discovered from Father Kevin's remarks last evening in his welcome and introduction, I'm just beginning my tenure as lecturer in New Testament here. It should not take me too long to remember everyone's names. I believe that in total there are about forty five of you in the three year cycle."

He continued, "I'll be distributing a few photo copied sheets outlining some of the details of this course including bibliographies and a course outline as well as our schedule of classes. That schedule is also posted in the glass case in the main foyer in the event you need to refer to it. I've read documents with regard to your personal information so I have a somewhat sketchy idea of who is who. Also, in the information that I'll be circulating you will find notes about the various papers and class work that will occur during the year. With regard to my lectures, I hope that you will feel free at any time to ask questions simply by raising your hand. I'm sure that we will have a productive and pleasant time exploring New Testament studies."

"For the initial period—until about the end of September—I plan to present an introduction to the documents of the New Testament—to look at the question of origins, types of parchments and scrolls and some of the issues of dating and language. Possibly you have, as I did years ago, the notion that the Scriptures simply existed as one book in leather covers from the very beginning. You will find that there has been an evolution—especially during the first four centuries—during which the Bible developed into its present day manifestation, and we will begin this morning with some of the conditions that are associated with the earliest days of the Church."

"Now, before I launch forth, are there any questions you might want to ask?"

One hand went up and Justin acknowledged saying, as he glanced at the class list, "Yes, Jeremy—I believe I'm right, am I not—Jeremy Clarke? Jeremy said, "Yes, Father, you are quite right. My question has to do with class work and term papers. I know that some of us have computers, word processors or typewriters, but if not, is there any alternative?"

"Good question Jeremy. I should have anticipated that. Well, first of all, with papers, I'll be happy to accept them in longhand, providing that it is legible, or done on a typewriter, but there are also a number of computers in the library equipped with printers and they all have the major word processing programmes. Heaven only knows, I'd be quite lost without my computer. Writing is made so much easier with them. So there are a number of alternatives and I dare say it shouldn't prove to be a problem for anyone."

"Thank you Father," Jeremy responded, "I'm sure we will all find our way around the place before very long."

"Good, and I'm sure that we will all value our time together here in this rather special atmosphere. Now, if there are no further questions I'll begin with the background information on my

Introduction to the New Testament."

✠

As the other two classes began their initial sessions Justin found the seminarians to be receptive to his approach and he gradually learned their names and became engrossed in the particular portions of the New Testament assigned to the second and third years. As well as the study of texts there was the Greek component that applied to each year. This proved to be the most challenging thing, as Justin had not really done much work with Greek since his own seminary years. However, he found it thought provoking and rather interesting. With the first year students it was of course, for most of them a first encounter with Greek and it involved learning vocabulary and grammar. With the other two years it was an occasion to look at Greek texts and to do class translation work, which was a little tedious and slow at times. It often resulted in the very practical discovery that there are times when the translations heard in chapel or in the course of reading scripture are challenged or at least discussed.

Mealtimes in the Seminary refectory were always a pleasure for Justin. It seemed at times that many of the seminarians clamoured to find places near him and to engage in conversation, which he quite enjoyed. He had noticed that on occasion Marc could not find a place at Justin's table and they would often share a knowing glance as Marc moved on. Marc knew that he couldn't dominate Justin's time, but they both realized that there was a growing bond between them, and that it was increasing as time went by. They had actually discussed that and agreed that they must be rather cautious—not that anything untoward was happening but simply so that there was no cause for anyone to entertain thoughts of favouritism. In truth, there were numbers of students who often talked and socialized with Justin. He was likeable and outgoing, which is all a part of the gifts that a priest needs to cultivate. Justin felt that he was in a very good space teaching and being involved with the Benedictine Community and he cherished it thoroughly.

ELEVEN

On an evening in the dead of winter Justin and Marc went for a relaxing stroll and discussion along a country road after Night Prayers and after the Great Silence had begun. They felt that they weren't intruding on anyone else's space and the sky was clear with a canopy of stars and a crescent moon. Marc wanted to raise a few questions about what the scripture class that day had introduced but had not really reached any definite conclusions. After a long period of silence Marc finally said, "Father, have you ever wondered about some of the historical questions that seem to remain unanswered with respect to St. Paul's life?"

"Well," Justin responded sotto voce, "Yes, as a matter of fact I've thought quite a lot about that. But, before we get into a long theological discussion about it, there is something I've wanted to say to you for some time." Justin took a little time thinking about just how he could frame his remarks. Finally, after several moments of silence, he looked at Marc and said, "We have become good friends Marc and I'm thoroughly enjoying your company—can I ask you something rather personal? When we are alone would you feel at all comfortable calling me Justin rather than Father?

Marc smiled as he took hold of Justin's hand "I've entertained that very thought often—and yes, I'd like that Justin. I'm glad you brought that up. I have to say that I've become very fond of you, and I've wanted to express it but was a little afraid that I might offend you."

"Not at all Marc. It's interesting we have both been having similar thoughts."

"Come over here for a moment under the shadow of these elms," Marc said as he led Justin by the elbow. Once amongst the trees Marc faced Justin, brushed his cheek lightly with his fingers, drew closer and gently kissed Justin on the lips. Justin responded and their tongues explored in a beautiful moment of delight. Justin's arms enfolded Marc and he said in a whisper, "Thank you. You don't know how long I've dreamed of touching and holding you."

Marc giggled excitedly and whispered, "Me too!" They stood for a long time savouring the warmth and delight. "I think the question, or comments I was about to raise about St. Paul can wait for another time. In any case they were perhaps simply to have something to talk about as I enjoy being with you. I realize that we both must be very discreet about this and you must know that I'd never want to embarrass you."

"Thank you Marc, that is very sweet. I can't tell you how utterly wonderful it was to hold you and to feel your breath—it has been a very, very long time—and to hold your hand now is so lovely."

"Thank you—and I echo your thoughts. Would you think me a little silly if I told you that I felt a rather magical attraction for you from the moment we first met? You remember me coming up and introducing myself in the refectory."

"Yes, indeed, I remember that moment vividly. Actually, Marc, I had noticed you even before that evening in the refectory, and to be honest, I was feeling exactly the same way. Can you believe that?"

"Yes. I thought the feeling was mutual. And, when you think of it, we have been very good about it—after all, that first encounter was well over a year ago." Marc squeezed Justin's hand and laughed. "Perhaps we should head back to the Abbey—I think we've walked for more than an hour. I hope no one noticed us missing and breaking the Great Silence!"

Justin laughed and remarked, "Well, we haven't really been making a lot of noise, have we?"

They walked on in silence delighting in the starry canopy, one another's presence and the warmth they brought to each other.

Justin finally broke the reverie and whispered, "There are so many things to tell you Marc, and to ask you. But, we will have time for that. Before you know it this term will be over and after the summer you will be back here for your final year. I suppose that eventually we will evolve some way of keeping in touch and seeing each other. It certainly is not an easy thing, is it, with issues in the church being debated as they are?"

"You're so right—it does seem to be a frightening mess for people like us. But, we will weather it through, I'm sure."

They approached the Abbey buildings almost at midnight. There appeared to be no one in sight and almost all of the residence windows were in darkness. Marc went with Justin to his rooms for a moment so they could spend one more delicious moment before parting. Justin thought to himself what a very affectionate young man Marc was as he clung to him not wishing to let him go. Finally, they shared one last kiss and Marc slipped out into the hallway and went down the stairs and to his room.

Justin sat down on the chesterfield for a while before getting ready for bed. He was exhilarated and could not stop thinking about the enjoyable evening.

TWELVE

The remainder of the term passed by extremely quickly, it seemed. Justin found his teaching enjoyable—even exciting—and the seminarians appeared to be enthusiastic about the New Testament courses. They began to ask questions more frequently than before and discussions often spilled over into the hallways and refectory. It seemed obvious to Justin as he graded papers and examinations that there was a curiosity and an interest that he had not fully expected.

As May approached and the classes began to reach their end the student's minds turned to thinking about their summer placements. Bishop Halpin wrote to Marc suggesting that he would like to make him a deacon in the Abbey Church before the term ended. All was arranged and Marc was beginning to become quite excited. The ordinations of several deacons and priests took place near the beginning of June. The monastery was a rather busy place for a week or so with the ordinations and graduation. Justin was extremely happy for Marc and the other ordinands. It was a remarkable time for both the seminary and the monastery.

Soon the place was quiet again and Justin could begin to prepare for the next year's courses. During this period from mid-June to September, Justin would be taking an increasingly more active part in the life of the Community—both in the Abbey liturgy and in the day to day functioning of the monk's refectory, where he would assist with the serving and reading. When his week for reading came around he was happy to find that they were beginning to read a recent translation of the Venerable Bede's classic, *An Ecclesiastical History of the English Nation*. He rather delighted at the thought of it.

In the course of the refectory rota Justin assisted with the weekly teams of monks who were responsible for bringing out the trolleys bearing bread, soups and main dishes, pitchers of water and milk from the kitchen and serving these to the tables. He quite liked the quiet and order of the monastic life, but very often his thoughts wandered away from his duties to fantasies of Marc and what he must be doing in his placement in yet another London parish. No doubt Marc's letters would soon begin to arrive and Justin was elated as he contemplated it.

✠

Summer weather was quite pleasant which was a bonus and over the course of the two month's hiatus Justin was able to apply himself to his research and lecture planning in the solitude of the Abbey's tranquillity and he felt contented with his work of sketching out the next semester's shape. On occasion he would sit down with Father Basil to consult and ask for his opinion on various matters. He was glad that his mentor was of the opinion that he was doing a good job of following in his footsteps. They would sometimes spend hours discussing the overall purpose of presenting the New Testament to eager minds which would soon be out in parishes passing on their knowledge and understanding of the Church's teaching.

Several times during that summer Justin also met with Father Kevin and Abbot Placidus about the general picture of the courses he taught with relation to the preparation the seminarians were receiving. He was immensely pleased that everyone was so supportive and that he was fitting into the Community's rhythm.

✠

Summer seemed to fly by quickly and correspondence with Marc was frequent. It was an important lifeline for Justin, although his study and course preparation together with his involvement with the Abbey routine kept him occupied.

August was nearly at its end now and before Justin knew it the seminarians began arriving back at the Abbey for the beginning of the Michaelmas Term. He looked forward to Marc's return with enthusiasm and to hearing all about his work in the past summer's placement. Justin knew the priest in the parish where Marc had spent this summer and in fact had visited them both for a few hours whilst on a day trip to London for an appointment with Dr. Landsworth.

Marc arrived back at the Abbey in the afternoon on the Wednesday of that last week before classes began. Justin saw him from his window emerging from the taxi at the main seminary entrance. He looked so handsome in his tee shirt and jeans. One of the other seminarians from Marc's class met him and helped carry his cases up to his room. Justin managed to restrain himself, remaining calm and disciplined deciding that it might be best to wait and see Marc at dinner that evening.

He thought to himself, as he gazed from the window, how amazing it was that two years had now passed since he began teaching at the Abbey and that this year would be Marc's final year at Basingshore. His thoughts quite naturally projected themselves forward to the time when Marc would leave to be appointed to a parish somewhere in the diocese, and wistfully wondered what would ever become of their friendship.

During Vespers in the Abbey Church that evening Justin's eyes met Marc's and they shared a cautious smile. Anticipation was growing as Vespers came to a close and they were able to greet each other and walk to the seminarian's refectory in a cascade of chatter. Justin watched Marc's beaming smile and animated conversation from across the dinner table as he regaled the others with stories of his summer placement. He thought to himself how curious it was that the two month break had seemed brief to him considering all the work and preparation he had accomplished, and yet so long in another sense.

Father Kevin had arranged for a social occasion during the Saturday before classes began especially to welcome the new seminarians and to begin the term. It was a wine and cheese party with just the minimum of speeches involving all the seminarians and the monks and others who would be teaching during the year. Both Marc and Justin were well aware that they must not appear to be as close as they really were. In the course of such social occasions they made a point of circulating around even though there were many glances and smiles exchanged between them. They would have opportunity to talk and be together on their frequent walks in the countryside.

On a drizzly Monday morning classes began and the routine of the Seminary began with enthusiasm.

Justin was now in his stride and was quite enjoying the rhythm and pace of the study programme. The Seminary was indeed a busy place and before one could scarcely blink an eye two months had elapsed and it was time for some first term papers to be handed in and for tutorial sessions to commence where Justin and individual students would sit down and discuss the contents of their papers. He loved this one-on-one aspect of his teaching as it provided a more personal contact because the classroom experience, although essential, was by nature somewhat more removed. With the introductory Greek grammar classes for the first year students it was more of a group related experience. In the more advanced years the seminarians would engage more in-group translation. This also led to a deeper appreciation of scripture studies and the difficulties and nuances that scripture translators encounter.

Over the course of the past two months Marc and Justin had managed to take the occasional long walk, although they often walked at night in order not to arouse any concern amongst the other students or the monks. It was comforting though that other members of the teaching staff and students also engaged in discussions and spent time together.

THIRTEEN

On an evening in November Justin and Marc lingered over their after dinner coffee in the Seminarian's Refectory. Eventually everyone else had left and the kitchen staff was circulating around clearing up the tables.

"You know, Justin, I haven't really ever spoken much to you about my family, have I?"

"Not really. I suppose we have been pretty much caught up with school issues and of course, our own personal relationship. Naturally, I'd be interested in hearing more about your life outside of school and church."

"Well, as you probably already know from my records I was a convert from Anglicanism. That was some years ago now—when I was about eighteen years old. But, that isn't here nor there really. I grew up in the country on an estate, which has been in the family for centuries. I was home schooled as a child by Mama until I went up to Oxford. My father had died when I was very small and so Mama raised me—well, along with the staff. Unfortunately, about six years ago Mama passed on as well—loneliness I think. At that time I inherited everything. But, living there became quite a bore really and that is how I ended up here at Basingshore. During the summer I was able to take a day or two from my parish duties and went up to see how things were getting on at the house. Oh yes, I kept it—it's rather dear to me actually—and I keep a small staff to manage it."

"My goodness, Marc, I'm rather taken aback. It is amazing to me that during the past two years none of this has surfaced. I don't quite know what to say."

"You don't have to say anything Justin. I suppose that we have just been so engrossed in other things—and amongst them our friendship that I didn't want to throw in anything that might, well, complicate it."

"Well, my dear, you certainly have maintained a remarkable restraint."

Justin continued, "We have talked for quite some time. Soon it will be time for Compline. After that, would you want to go for a late evening walk? It is a clear night so it would be pleasant, although a little chilly, but we can bundle up."

"That would be delightful. I've longed to be close to you and to just touch you. So, after office we can slip away and perhaps walk down the road where we have gone before and perhaps linger in the wooded part."

"That will be nice, Marc. I'll meet you after Compline near the gatehouse."

Marc put on a warm wool cardigan under his cassock before Compline and after the office, when everyone had gone back to their quarters in silence, he quietly wandered down to the gatehouse and sat on the bench and waited for Justin. Soon a dark shape approached from the direction of the Seminary. Marc stood up and waited near the entrance way not quite sure if the figure was Justin or not—he was nervous about making an assumption in the darkness. As the person neared the crunch of the gravel on the dry roadway echoed against the gatehouse. Out of the darkness came the whispered "Marc, is that you?"

"Yes, just relax, no one seems to be around at all." Marc took Justin's arm as they began down toward the country road. "It is so nice to feel you close Justin."

"It is. We can take a nice long walk. I'm all caught up with my review of the mid-term papers and I'm prepared to face classes tomorrow so I can relax. Are you able to spend some time walking and chatting?"

"Yes, and I've been looking forward to being

with you again. We do keep busy with things here!"

"For certain," Justin remarked. "Since you told me about your family background and the estate I haven't been able to get it out of my mind for some reason. I hope you are comfortable about it—I suppose I am just a little astonished as it had never come into our conversations."

Marc smiled broadly and said, "Well, my Dear, I was just being a bit cautious, I don't know why. I suppose we are both wondering about the future and what might become of us. I'm sure things will sort out, or take their natural course," he added as he squeezed Justin's arm. They looked at each other fondly in the dim light and continued walking for some time in silence. Undoubtedly, they were both musing on just what the future would hold for them.

Finally after some silence Marc drew closer to Justin and whispered, "Let's not think about the future too much tonight and just enjoy being together."

Justin put his arm around Marc and kissed him lightly on the cheek with a smile and said, "You're right—we shouldn't dwell on things too much, but simply enjoy each other's company.

After a short silence Marc looked at Justin and asked, "Do you remember me once remarking about St. Paul's life and history?"

"Yes, I think I recall that we were going to save it for some future time."

"Well, perhaps this is as good a time as any to

unload something that has been, well, bothering me for some time—especially after last year when we delved into the Pauline Epistles."

"Oh, I hope I didn't create any difficulties for you during that course."

"No, it is not that at all. But, let me explain. Let's see, where should I begin? Well, I suppose that I have had some negative feelings about Paul for many years actually, which seems to be associated with some of the issues that are being rather hotly debated in the churches right now. To be brief, issues of women in the Church and also the hot button issue of gays in the Church. Of course, in Anglican circles and in a number of other churches it is the subject of huge debate. In the Catholic Church it is, of course, sort of an off limits subject, so to speak, but that is really another problem in itself."

"I know what you are saying, Marc, and I too have a lot of reservations about those issues."

Marc continued, "Really! Well, sparked by your course on St. Paul, I became rather interested in reading material on the historical dimensions of Paul's life and that made the problem even worse. I confess that I did read a lot of material that is not sanctioned by the Catholic Church, but that in itself made it all the more tempting."

"My Dear, I've also done that. I'm afraid there's nothing more tempting than the forbidden."

Marc continued, "I suppose there is something about my Anglican and Oxford background which says, in essence, that it is good to explore all possibilities and to understand the pros and cons of all questions. But, in this case it led me to explore Paul's life a little more deeply than is apparent in the scriptures. Part of the problem, of course, is contained in the Acts of the Apostles, which was probably written by Luke whose ear Paul must have bent, so to speak. Just from a historical point of view there are so many facts that simply don't add up. For instance, Paul claims in various places that he studied and lived in Jerusalem and according to dates, it must have been at the same time as Jesus, including when he was crucified, and yet Paul never even mentions any of that as contemporary knowledge. He claimed to have studied under Gamaliel but there seems to be no corroborating evidence of that fact either."

"True, true," Justin whispered.

"The only references to Paul knowing Jesus are his own visions or dreams. And then, there are the rather many ideas that Paul introduces which seem to contradict the Gospel accounts of Jesus' teaching —like male headship or dominance and his apparent criticism of gays which Jesus never even mentions. And then there are some rather strange opinions about men having short hair and women long hair, and things about hats, which don't seem to have much relevance to anything at all. I'm sorry Justin, I'm rambling on, aren't I!"

"That's alright Marc. I can assure you I've

thought about those things too. However, I suppose we have to remember that Paul *did* systematize and explain a lot about salvation and justification in addition to those questionable things you refer to. I mean his thought makes it clear that he believed that through Jesus we have come to know God's justice as love rather than as wrath, and this has greatly informed our understanding of God. Now, I realize that many Christians still seem to prefer to see God from a crude legalistic perspective."

"Yes, I suppose," Marc conceded, "but then there are other things which I really have problems with—like how Paul had to be the best in everything—a Hebrew amongst Hebrews; even a Pharisee no less; a Roman citizen; speaking in tongues more than anyone else. It even comes across to me like he perhaps had some psychological issues."

"Yes, there is that, I have to admit?"

"And to top it all off there were his problems and disagreements with the Jerusalem Church and with Peter and James and others. He was even summoned by James to come to Jerusalem to explain himself."

"I know Marc—and what you say certainly does hint of problems that go even deeper. For instance, there is the whole question of Paul's actual presentation of the doctrine of the atonement, which is definitely one rooted in the idea of penal substitution, which is also one of the principal notions that the protestant evangelical segment of

Christianity espouses, even though through the history of the Church there have been four or five different theological explanations of the atonement —of course, no single theory is ever able to adequately and tidily explain such a mystery."

"Right, and that plays right into the hands of those who wish to paint God as a vengeful and punishing despot—one who demands a ransom," Marc countered.

"Well, my Dear," Justin added, "and there are many Catholics who also prefer that sort of religion. But, unfortunately for us, it also boils down to the fact that Rome and the Magisterium prevent open discussion of such things—it is really an approach that we dare not take. Can you imagine what would happen if I allowed, or even encouraged, such discussion here in my classes? The Church police— meaning the Office of the Congregation for the Doctrine of the Faith—would be summoning me to Rome in the twinkling of an eye."

"I realize that, Justin. I guess it is just one of those things that more progressive people have to accept and keep mum about, isn't it!"

"Yes, you're right—and besides that there is the whole question of the canon of holy scripture and which documents were to be included and which were to be left out. And the sheer volume of Paul's writing, which is almost half of the New Testament, was accepted in the early centuries. At this point in history, to raise issues about that would be total anathema—especially as the whole of Christendom is amazingly unified on that one question. I must admit, at times I've wondered how on earth the early Fathers gave Paul such prominence. But, listen my Sweet, let's not get too carried away with these things for the present—I mean like tonight—let's just enjoy our walk and being together."

Justin put his arm around Marc and nuzzled his neck as they were nearing the grove of trees where they had kissed. Once in the shadows Justin put his arms around Marc and drew him close, kissing him tenderly. After a lingering embrace Justin looked into Marc's eyes and whispered softly, "You know, I love you very much, Marc."

Marc giggled a bit and then said, "Yes, and I love you too. I'm sorry I giggled—but the thought that ran through my head was, 'Is that a gun in your pocket'.

Justin laughed and said, "You little devil—I love it!" ... And kissed him again.

FOURTEEN

For the next few weeks Justin's thoughts were quite distracted by images of Marc and what would become of their friendship once Marc had been ordained to the priesthood and posted somewhere in a parish. He was able to cope with the teaching and it was really in those times when he was busy with his work that his thoughts about Marc rested. The thought of Marc leaving the Seminary was simply too hazardous to contemplate at the moment. This was actually the first time in his life that he had loved so profoundly and enjoyed its reciprocation. He loved his work and had an extremely strong sense of his vocation. He delighted in being a priest. This was also perhaps the first time in his ordained life that he had ever felt such a strong sense of distraction.

During the next few weeks Justin had a number of interviews scheduled with students wishing to discuss aspects of their recent papers and a few who

Justin needed to talk with regarding their grasp of certain issues. It was, however, a long standing tradition at Basingshore that after papers were submitted every seminarian would have the opportunity to spend some time with his tutor in order to share ideas on a personal level.

In the first week of interviews Justin found it refreshing to speak privately with two of the students who, for the most part, were unusually quiet during class discussion. One was a north country lad, Jeremy, whose accent reminded Justin a little of Nigel's, which brought back many memories. Justin was beginning to get over the tragic aspects of Nigel's demise and his thoughts were now mostly centred on Nigel's gentleness and quiet sense of humour. He thought to himself how very much Marc had provided a new focus in his personal life and was reminded just how much Marc meant to him.

The other student was in his late twenties, and also quiet and self-assured. He was planning to join the Benedictines when he finished his seminary training this year and remain at Basingshore. One of his interests was in music and particularly the organ. Justin recalled how pleased Father Kevin was that there would be someone to take on that aspect of the Abbey's life as the current organist was getting on in years.

✠

Near the end of those weeks of interviews, on a Friday evening when Justin was feeling particularly pleased with how things had progressed with the students he was having dinner in the Seminarian's Refectory. He was sitting at a table for six and amongst the five seminarians were Marc who seemed never to be very concerned about being seen in Justin's company frequently; Ronald Granger, a first year student who was from Ireland; Romeo Mendoza, a Filipino who had come to Britain and to Basingshore to study; and two other first year students, John and Eric who were both from London. The dinner had been pleasant and everyone's spirits seemed to be buoyed up being Friday evening and the end of classes for the week. Justin was also relaxed because the week had come to an end and he was delighting in being with these eager students. The conversation had been clever and quite interesting during the course of the dinner. As they sat finishing their custard and coffee—and without any hint of what was about to explode—Eric innocently made a remark about the writing of term papers on the computer, remarking about the immense availability of materials and ideas on the internet. Justin found that comment rather interesting and casually remarked, "I know what you mean Eric. You know Teilhard de Chardin more than fifty years ago predicted that such a network of thought, which he called the *noosphere* would evolve to draw people together."

Marc's eyes widened as he watched Romeo's expression from the opposite side of the table. Romeo went red in the face and had such a look of fury when Justin mentioned Teilhard. His eyes bulged so that it looked like he might become violent.

Finally he burst and blurted out, "Father, how can you even mention him? You know better than we do that he was inhibited by the Vatican and that he is considered to be a heretic. He denied Catholic teaching about sin and proclaimed a kind of pantheism in his writings."

John and Eric appeared to be shocked that a seminarian would speak so angrily and critically to Father Justin. Marc, of course, was also surprised at Romeo's outburst, but knowing Justin so well and being more liberally situated, he didn't find the mention of Teilhard at all shocking. There was rather a hush after the burst of anger as Justin considered how to respond to Romeo.

"Romeo," he said hesitatingly, "I realize what you say is thought to be true to many, but you surely know that Father Teilhard's writings have quite a following in most European countries and around the world. He was able to frame theological ideas in terms that are consistent with modern science and technology. You probably also realize that there are Teilhard de Chardin Associations all around the world. I know that many of his ideas are complex

and difficult to comprehend and that is surely one of
the reasons why the Congregation for the Doctrine
of the Faith originally made its decision. They
seemed to be more concerned that he might be
devaluing the idea of sin and especially the concept
of original sin which was not really well founded in
scripture, but which came more from the theology of
St. Augustine of Hippo and others."

Romeo was calming down a little at this point
and he remarked slightly more rationally, "But,
Father, the inhibition on his writing is still enforced
by the Vatican and the Magisterium."

"I understand that Romeo, but at the same time
I'd point out that my reference to Teilhard was in
the context of a simple dinner table conversation
and not as material contained in my official teaching
curriculum. It is true that I, personally, have a great
admiration for Teilhard and his visionary thinking,
as do many other Catholics. I feel sorrow that the
Church is so often slow in recognizing genius, as also
was the case with people like Galileo. But, I do feel
that it is healthy and natural that we should be able
to have a table conversation like this and express our
opinions. I should also point out that the Holy
Father quite recently made some glowing comments
about Father Teilhard's life and work, although
unfortunately he did not take the next logical step
and lift the inhibition on his writings. I should add
here that many Jesuits, some of whom were very
much in support of Teilhard, like Henri de Lubac,

actually overlap with Teilhard de Chardin and quite possibly knew and respected him. But, as I said earlier, I believe this sort of discussion is good and should not be feared."

The conversation seemed to trail off after Justin's calm comments and perhaps Romeo thought better about continuing to argue, especially as he really knew very little about the depths of the issue. Before long they were finishing up their coffee, clearing up the table and excusing themselves. Fortunately, it came to a peaceable end—at least for the present.

Marc noticed Justin lingering near the entrance to the Abbey Church after Compline and approached. He whispered, "Justin, do you feel like a stroll?"

"I certainly do. I was hoping you would spot me and suggest it."

They wandered silently toward the Gate House and once out on the road and away from the buildings Justin nudged Marc and said impishly, "Well, that was a little awkward at table, wasn't it!"

"Well, my Dear, you said what you believe and what is true with sincerity—what more could one expect?"

"Yes, I know, but I feel a little sorry for Romeo. I realize that he has a simple faith and a conception that everything just fits together like a jigsaw puzzle with no pieces left over and no blank spots. Although, I have to admit that I find it difficult to comprehend how people like Romeo keep any sort of ordered theological perspective. I mean it puzzles me because people like him often seem to be able to maintain an ultraconservative Catholic base and yet to have at the same time no difficulty embracing some odd mixtures of superstition—as is fairly common in parts of the West Indies as well as in Africa to say nothing of the extreme Holy Week practices in the Philippines. I suppose that when I was young and just beginning to grapple with theological thought I was somewhat like Romeo. How were you in coping with such things when you began?"

Marc thought for a moment and then replied, "I suppose that because of my background and my exposure to discussing and contesting ideas at Oxford, it wasn't such a novel idea. Mind you, I can recall a time when Father Basil was teaching Mark's Gospel in my first year when I began to have the feeling that the bottom was dropping out—especially when we got near the end of the Gospel and encountered the question of the spurious ending with its inconsistency with the rest of the document. But, I got over that, fortunately."

"I quite understand, and of course, I'm well aware that I'm going to run into that exact same difficulty with Romeo when we approach that point. I even vaguely anticipated such a reaction from some students when I was preparing my notes for first year classes."

Marc took Justin's arm and gave it a squeeze. "Don't worry now—just wait and see where things go. Anyway, it is unavoidable—you have to do what you have to do."

"Well, yes, I think you're right—I just hope Romeo doesn't cause trouble for me—this is only my third year here."

"Don't fret, we will see things through. I too have some questions about my situation. Bishop Halpin wrote to me recently about ordaining me to the Priesthood. He wants me to go to London sometime soon to talk about possibilities. And in due course he will inevitably raise the question about a parish appointment somewhere—hopefully not too far away. As I believe I mentioned to you at some point, I know the Bishop quite well—we were actually quite friendly a few years ago, so I feel quite comfortable talking with him."

"Yes, Marc, I do remember you casually remarking about the Bishop," he responded, recalling that Marc's reference to the Bishop had been rather vague, though perhaps somewhat intriguing. He also thought how wonderful and supportive Marc was. He really was wiser than his years and it was so refreshing to be able to confide in him and to vent.

FIFTEEN

Several days later Justin had spent rather a busy day with an extra session involving his second year students. When classes finally ended he went by his mail slot in the main hallway and found that there were two letters waiting for him and a note from Kevin asking if they might meet after dinner in the faculty lounge. It indicated that he need not respond if he was able to meet. Glancing at his watch he saw that it was a little over half an hour until Vespers so he went to his rooms and had a brief lie down and then washed up and went down to the church.

Dinner in the seminarians refectory was quiet for a change. Marc was involved in a discussion with some of his classmates and Justin was alone for the first few minutes until he was joined by a student who wanted to talk about an issue that had arisen during a class that morning. It was rather a nice change he thought, having a quiet dinner. He glanced around to observe the various small groups of students and noticed that Romeo was sitting with his friends discussing what sounded from the distance to be a sports event. Perhaps it was their upcoming cricket match on Saturday.

Finishing his coffee, Justin organized his crockery, deposited the tray on the dirty dish trolley at the back of the refectory, and went up to the faculty lounge to browse some magazines as he waited for Kevin to appear. It was not a long wait. Father Kevin entered, greeted Justin, and took a seat nearby. The lounge was empty except for the two of them.

"Well," began Kevin, "how are things going for you? It's been some time since we talked at any length."

"Yes, it has. But to answer your question, things are going well I believe. I'm quite enjoying my classes and the students seem to be responding well. In a way it's hard to believe that I'm into my third year here. The seminarians seem to be working hard at their studies and there have been few difficulties with term papers and the normal academic routines. There are a few who seem to have a struggle with Greek, but that is quite normal, I think. I find my individual tutorial sessions with students most interesting—and, as well, it is a wonderful way to get to know them."

"I'm so glad that you are enjoying the teaching and being here at the Abbey. Just in passing, I've noticed that you seem to have a close relationship with Marc Sinclair."

"Yes, you're quite right, I do. He is very affable and interesting. We have had some quite fascinating conversations about course material and life in the Church in general."

"I hate to sound inquisitive or concerned, Justin," Kevin remarked hesitatingly as he weighed his words, "but do be careful—if you understand what I mean. I'm just recalling our student days and, well, you know how well we know each other. But, Justin, that is just an aside. The reason I actually wanted to chat with you is completely unrelated. I had a visit from Romeo Mendoza a few days ago and he was quite agitated."

"Oh no," Justin remarked, his eyes widening and posture stiffening. "The Teilhard de Chardin discussion, if you can call it a discussion!"

Kevin hesitated a moment then said, "Do you want to recount what caused his reaction?"

"Well, certainly. By the way there were about six of us sitting at dinner in the seminarian's refectory, so there were others who overheard our conversation. Yes, Romeo did get rather angry. Well, I'll try and condense it to give you the drift. One of the young men, I can't actually remember who at the moment, made a comment about writing his term paper on the computer and made a comment about how marvellous it was that information and resources were so easily accessed on the internet. And it was then that I made a comment about Teilhard and how he had predicted decades ago that someday there would be a sort of network of thought and understanding which he called the 'noosphere'. Well, that was when Romeo lost his temper. He angrily rebuked me, to the surprise of the others, and informed me that the Holy Office had prohibited de Chardin's writing and that he was a heretic and so on. I tried to calm him by explaining that I was well aware of all of that, but that there were many who held Teilhard to have been a visionary man of great depth. I also pointed out that my comment—not meant to be at all confrontational—was made innocently during a dinner conversation and had not been taught or even alluded to during my teaching. He seemed at the time to calm down and compose himself and I hoped that he would realize that it was a tempest in a teapot. However, I suppose I was wrong."

Kevin looked across at Justin pensively for a moment or two, then said, "Well, that certainly is much the way he recounted it as well, although during our chat he again became a little emotional and blurted out something about writing to his bishop about it. I hope that doesn't happen—we don't want you becoming another Hans Küng, do we!

"Well," Justin said shaking his head ruefully, "I'd personally take that to be a compliment, however, I certainly don't want to bring any discredit or embarrassment upon Basingshore."

"Don't worry, Justin," Kevin said with a twinkle in his eye, "If some bishop complains to the Vatican we'll probably all be long departed before they ever get around to doing anything about it."

✠

Justin tried to put his mind to some serious reading that evening after his meeting with Father Kevin but it was a rather useless exercise as his thoughts were distracted by the conversation they had had about Romeo and Teilhard de Chardin. And what was Kevin driving at with his remark about the friendship with Marc? He thought that their behaviour had always been discreet. Of course, he realized perfectly well that to a person who might be so inclined, a simple smile or eye movement could reveal one's innermost thoughts. He even wondered if he might not be getting a little paranoid about his relationship with Marc. He longed for the next occasion when he and Marc could walk and chat. Marc was always so positive and relaxed—that was one of the things that attracted him to Marc. As he mused about the refectory confrontation with Romeo he wondered why many people in the Church were so keen on being judgmental and prone to a simplistic faith that is black and white. With that mind set, he thought, it is certainly no wonder why Teilhard's ideas disturbed Romeo so much, as indeed they had ruffled the feathers of the Curia.

Eventually, after going over all of these interconnected thoughts in his mind Justin was able to relax a little with a nightcap and resume his reading for a while before retiring for the evening. Tomorrow would be another demanding day, but at least he could look forward to seeing Marc, if only for a few fleeting moments.

SIXTEEN

It had been a rather busy week what with the teaching responsibilities, staff meetings and other concerns, but Justin was glad that Friday had finally arrived. He dealt with the afternoon classes during which the subject of the next term paper was discussed. He had the reassuring feeling that things were on schedule and organized. At dinner that evening he was surrounded by the usual group who seemed intent on engaging him in conversation, which of course, he loved. Marc was naturally one of that group, however Romeo was now quite obviously disengaging from them—or, at least from Justin. He sat in another part of the refectory looking a little downtrodden talking with another student who was also known for his conservatism. When the meal and the clearing up were finished, Marc lingered in the hallway until Justin appeared. They both stood for a few minutes at the bulletin board perusing the notices and schedules. Finally, Justin said quietly,

"It's been a long and busy week for me. How has your week been?"

"Well, quite busy, but the usual thing," Marc answered in a hushed tone. "Do you fancy a walk after Compline tonight? After all, the weekend is upon us."

"Yes, that would be pleasant. If you hadn't suggested it, I'd have."

"Alright, let's meet near the gatehouse after chapel."

"Good," said Justin, "I'll see you there."

✠

It was another of those mostly clear nights with a few clouds scudding across the sky and a crescent moon peeking through occasionally. Justin approached the gatehouse and could see that Marc had already arrived and was standing in the shadows. He approached cautiously, just in case it was someone else. Marc smiled at Justin in the darkness as they launched out down the road.

"This is nice," Marc said as he took Justin's arm, "I've missed you."

"I have as well, and I've a little gossip to pass on to you."

Marc laughed quietly, "I have a little news too. But, do go on, I always enjoy a bit of gossip."

Justin smiled knowingly as he glanced at Marc's bright eyes and continued, "Well, Father Kevin wanted to see me a few nights ago to discuss how things were going, so we met after dinner for a talk. In the course of his introductory chitchat he casually mentioned that he had noticed our 'friendship' and seemed a bit concerned about it. You know, a staff member and a student. At the time I wondered why he was noticing it at all, but presumed that it was simply from our conversations at table and perhaps our obvious delight in each other. He expressed a little concern for me. At least that is what he said. I wondered if someone had seen us leaving the grounds late at night on one of these walks."

Marc seemed rather happy to hear what Justin was saying and added, "Well, even if someone has noticed us together out here, we haven't done anything that exciting—unless they saw us in a fond embrace—but it has always been in the complete blackness of the elms. Anyway, we haven't done anything that outrageous, have we?"

"Well, no, not really!"

Marc continued with an impish tone, "But one of these times we might, you know!"

They dissolved momentarily in giggles, and Justin was charmed because the thought had naturally crossed his mind as well.

For a time they walked on in silence savouring one another's company. Justin was indeed enthralled with Marc and it was obvious that the feeling was mutual.

Eventually, Justin broke the reverie and

remarked, "But, that was just Father Kevin's introductory remark—he eventually got around to his real concern and it turned out to be the Romeo issue. You will find this amusing! I'm referring to the dinner conversation where I innocently mentioned Teilhard de Chardin and Romeo went ballistic. Apparently he went to talk to Father Kevin and recounted the conversation—or, as I suspect, parts of it. And to top it all off he was threatening to write to his bishop about it—*me*, I take that to mean."

"Really!" Marc snorted, almost laughing. "And I don't suppose he explained that this was in the context of a dinner table conversation rather than in a lecture?

"Well, I'm not certain about that," Justin offered, "but I did recount to Kevin the way I understood the encounter to have unfolded—including my comments about the popular interest in Teilhard in segments of the Church. But, Kevin didn't seem too concerned about it. I think he just wanted to let me know what had happened."

"I'm glad he talked with you—even just to convey that."

Justin laughed and said, "He actually made the comment that even if Romeo's bishop took this to the Holy Office in Rome they would probably take eons to ever follow it up. I think more than anything Kevin just found it amusing. After all, he is bound to have figured Romeo out by now."

They walked on in silence for several minutes,

neither of them being very worried about Romeo or what the Principal thought. Surely it would soon slip into the past and be forgotten. Marc pressed Justin's arm all of a sudden as he remembered some of his own news. "Oh, Justin, I almost forgot to tell you—I have an appointment with Bishop Halpin in two weeks. I'm going to go up to London for a consultation with him. I'm sure it will centre on my ordination to the priesthood and where that might take place as well, perhaps, about my first parish placement. It is so exciting, although I'm concerned about our seeing each other, but I'm sure things will work for us."

"I hope so Marc—I've become very attached to you, you know!"

"Yes, I do know my Love, and likewise for me."

The rest of the walk back to the Abbey was silent as they were both thinking about how the future might unfold for them. Justin was thinking about how pleasant the past three years had been and how very much he adored Marc. Marc's thoughts were racing ahead and exploring the possibilities that might await him—a parish appointment in London or perhaps in one of the rural areas of the Archdiocese—thoughts of travelling by train to visit Justin. How was this next transition going to manifest itself? At least he was not feeling stress about meeting with the Bishop as he knew him quite well and that he was quite aware of the personal dynamics that were at play in Marc's life.

They soon reached the gatehouse and lingered for a few moments in the shadows as they bid each other goodnight and then went on their way to their rooms in the Seminary Block.

✠

Weeks seemed to flash past like days in the busy flow of lectures and seminars, which was good both for Justin and Marc. Being so occupied with work and studies was merciful as it kept their minds from dwelling too much on prospects for the future.

Marc took the train into London on a Friday afternoon for his visit with Bishop Halpin and planned to return to Basingshore late that evening. It would be helpful to know what the Bishop was planning. Perhaps he and Justin would be able to settle down a little and have some idea of what the future held for them. It was both an anxious time as well as an exciting adventure, which was taking on new dimensions the more they thought about it. There were times when Justin felt like it was all a whirlwind even though the relationship had evolved over the space of several years.

Justin thought often on that Friday evening about Marc and his meeting with the Bishop and knew that it would not be long before he would hear all about it. Being so well acquainted with the Basingshore to London train schedule, he was well aware that Marc would probably arrive back at the

Abbey quite late. He decided to retire about eleven thirty after a pleasant evening of reading. He would wait to see Marc the next day when they could spend some leisure time talking and discuss the encounter with the Bishop.

SEVENTEEN

Breakfast on Saturday mornings was a little later than usual in order to give the Seminarians a bit of a sleep in. Justin bathed and went to Lauds in the Abbey Church after which he strolled over to the Seminary Refectory. There were not very many at breakfast yet. He took a tray and selected some cereal, toast and a coffee. Sitting down at a corner table, he removed his breakfast from the tray while behind him he could hear a few of the students arriving. Marc was amongst them and he came over to say good morning.

"How are you? I had a very good trip yesterday afternoon. But, right now I'll get some breakfast and join you."

"Alright—I'll be interested to hear all about it."

Marc returned after a few minutes, and glancing around at the other students, he said, "Before anyone else joins us, I just want to let you know that I had an extremely interesting talk with the Bishop and I want to tell you all about it—but it is quite complex and lengthy—so, perhaps we could take one of our evening strolls tonight and I can explain it all."

"Certainly," Justin rejoined, "I'll be anxious to hear what happened."

"I think we'll need an extra long walk," Marc whispered, which made Justin all the more curious. He continued, "Anyway, I have a lot of work to do today as you probably do as well and then we can relax tonight and go into all the details."

"Well, I can hardly wait," Justin remarked.

Marc added, "It's certainly information that we daren't let anyone here overhear."

That certainly got a wide-eyed response from Justin and the remark lingered in his mind for the rest of the day. He was pleased the way Marc was so dramatic and had such a flair for hyperbole. Little did he realize just how surprising this meeting with the Bishop would prove to be.

Preparation for next week's classes occupied Justin for the whole day and he was actually pleased that Marc had suggested waiting until the evening to discuss his meeting with Bishop Halpin in London.

✠

The night was dark and somewhat foreboding as Justin entered the Abbey Church for Compline and his thoughts about a walk afterward were somewhat conflicted. Perhaps the rain would hold off but it might be wise to take an umbrella when they ventured forth. Taking his place in choir his glance connected momentarily with Marc's and he was gratified to see his warm smile. After the office Justin found Marc down by the Gatehouse noticing that he too had brought his umbrella, but there was not yet any sign of rain. They set off down the road, Justin giving Marc's arm a little squeeze as he said, "I'm so glad you had a safe journey and that you're back. I know it was only a day trip, but my thoughts were with you."

"Thank you. I was thinking about you as well. Everything went quite smoothly. I'll try to explain everything that we discussed. It is a little involved but let me see if I can keep everything in order. First of all I should explain a bit about my past as far as the Bishop is concerned. I think I once remarked that we had some sort of association or friendship."

"Yes, I recall that. I've wondered about it several times. You did leave it a little vague."

"I know. I didn't feel at the time that there was much point in getting very specific about it—not that there is very much to tell, actually. I met the Bishop socially somewhere a number of years ago— before I converted. I suppose that he was partly the reason I was received into the Catholic Church. Where to begin? Well, we met at a social event in the country north of London. We found ourselves getting quite involved in a conversation, and were rather enjoying the talk. I found him to be congenial and interesting and he was obviously caught up in the chat as well. Because it was a social event we couldn't really detach from it and spend a lot of time talking, so before parting we agreed to keep in touch and perhaps meet again to talk, which we did. He was rather obviously interested in me and I quite liked him, but perhaps not quite to the same degree. But, we did meet to talk and socialize numbers of times. And, there were eventually a few, shall I say, intimate moments. He was very civil and kind, and to make a long story shorter, I ended up here and, well, you know the rest."

"I see—that's very interesting. And I gather it leads to more?"

"Yes, it certainly does. That is just the beginning. Let me try and flesh out where the conversation went. First, before we got into the most interesting part of our discussion the Bishop explained that he had made plans to ordain me to the Priesthood here at the Abbey in June, and that he wished to appoint me as an assistant to a priest in a London parish. The exact details have not yet been worked out so I'm a bit vague on that.

During our talk I found an appropriate moment to talk about you and basically told him that we have developed a very special relationship. I hope you don't mind, my Dear—I just thought it was an opportune moment and I seized it. The Bishop then opened up considerably and seemed to be quite happy for both of us. I think he was particularly happy for you which mystified me a little, but not enough to cause me to worry about the direction it was taking."

"Well, no, I certainly don't mind—but I have a sense that there is much more to come. Where did the conversation go from there?"

"Here is where it gets even more interesting, and I'll try to simplify things as I go. He had a few suggestions to make but wishes to talk to you and the Abbey before taking anything further."

"Oh, now you've got me intrigued!"

"Yes, my Dear, now let me pick up on his suggestions. First of all you need to remember that he knows me quite well including my background and about the house in the country. He suggests that I continue with his idea of serving a curacy in an, as yet unspecified, London parish for a year to gain experience, and that you continue to teach here for another year. At about that time a member of the Benedictine Community will be returning from his studies in Rome. He could then take your place in the New Testament scripture and Greek departments. Of course, the Bishop needs to talk with you, Father Kevin and the Abbot about all of this scheming."

"My God, you are a busy one—and dare I ask what happens after all of that?"

"Yes, you may. Obviously, there is quite a bit more to come. He was very interested in trying to assist us—I mean, like our staying together, and he knows all about Ashley Hall, which I haven't told you much about, but which is the house I inherited from Mama. And Ashley is fairly close to several small parishes, which don't have any accommodation for clergy. He knew that I had opted to retain the house and property and he thought that we might live there and have vehicles provided for travel around the parishes. I know this is just in the preliminary stages, but it might work very well for everyone all round, and we would be together. It seems like a dream to me!"

"Very interesting—that certainly gives us a lot to think about."

Marc's brow furrowed a bit as he tried to assess Justin's reaction and then he continued, "I hope I haven't overstepped my bounds or offended you by talking so candidly with the Bishop."

"No, certainly not. You seem to have quite a rapport with him and I believe you would know just how candid you could be with him. It is all quite dreamlike, my Dear."

"I thought so too," replied Marc. "I could think of nothing else on the return trip to the Abbey last evening. I was also thinking that we should go for a visit to Ashley so that you can see for yourself what we are talking about. I can tell that you have questions, which is understandable. I can only say at this point that Ashley is not a little cottage! But we do need to go for a visit in order to put things into perspective."

Justin nodded in agreement and added, "And that would mean that we would still have a year more or less apart."

"Yes," Marc replied, "but London is not all that far away and we will see each other from time to time. We'll have to make those times special!

"Yes, my Pet...and it is a lot of material to digest all at once, but it does sound exciting, and it will be very good to have that time to prepare ourselves."

Marc giggled and replied, "Yes, and the Bishop also mentioned about having that year of transition because, as he said, 'It would make the whole arrangement appear much more natural'."

Justin put his arm around Marc and gave him a kiss on the cheek. "It is all rather overwhelming, isn't it?"

"It certainly is—and I'm glad that I told the Bishop about our situation. He did seem so interested and willing to do what he could to let this play out. He is quite fond of you Justin as you probably know—it is almost like a kind of indebtedness—I'm not sure I understand it, but you probably do."

Justin smiled and thought for a few moments before replying, "Well, I'm glad that he feels kindly toward me, but I must say, I don't understand why either. Perhaps it's just his nature."

They walked on in silence for some time letting the full weight of this adventure sink in. Eventually,

Marc leaned his head on Justin's shoulder and whispered, "You know, Justin, the first time I saw you when you arrived at the Abbey I felt eerily convinced that something wonderful was about to happen between us—I know that sounds silly and impetuous, but the feeling was so vivid."

EIGHTEEN

Justin passed by the Gatehouse in his usual vigorous stride late one evening, his Capa Negra flapping in the chill breeze. He frequently ventured out for some fresh air on sleepless nights and his thoughts were usually focussed upon issues involving his classes and students, but also upon Marc. It was fall now and the brown and yellow hues of the heath were a pleasant change after the unusually hot and pleasant summer.

His thoughts recapped the flurry of events that had transpired during the past three months—almost too much to assimilate. It began with Marc's ordination as a Priest in the Abbey Church at the end of term. He was one of five ordained by Bishop Halpin at the Abbey and the crowd of friends and family members was huge. Justin's thoughts lingered for a time on that happy day. Marc had no family members present—in fact Justin had the impression that he really did not have any close family members. He rather thought of himself as Marc's only 'family' and he relished the thought. The ordination was followed a few days later with the Seminary graduation exercises. Many festivities and parties occurred at that time in addition to bidding those leaving the Seminary farewell as they went their various ways.

Marc and the others who were leaving Seminary for their new parishes spent a few days packing their books and belongings and making preparations for the moving of their lives to new adventures. Most of them were destined for London or its environs and they had arranged for a van to deal with the many cartons and valises. It was a time of a certain amount of anxiety for Justin and Marc, as they knew that they would not be seeing each other on a daily basis as they had for the past several years.

Following the ordinations, at a reception in the Seminary Refectory, Bishop Halpin came over to Justin who was standing near the buffet table. Justin had just picked up a glass of Sauvignon and noticing that the Bishop did not have a drink offered to get him one. They were alone for only a few minutes before someone else wanted to talk with the Bishop; however, they did have enough time for Bishop Halpin to suggest a meeting with Justin at his London office sometime during the next few weeks. They soon agreed on a date and time and duly marked it in their pocket agendas. Justin recalled how very accommodating and clever the Bishop was when they met. He outlined his thoughts about what might become of him and Marc, and it tallied more or less exactly with what Marc had recounted —that Justin should continue to teach at the Abbey for another year and that Marc should spend a year as an assistant at the parish of St. Benedict in London. He talked about the monk who would then replace him in New Testament studies when he returned from Rome in about a year's time. The Bishop was extremely candid about the plan which he had hatched with Marc about the two of them living on Marc's estate and shepherding several small parishes nearby. It would be beneficial to the Diocese, the parishes involved and of course to Marc and Justin. It simply made good sense, and waiting for a year to elapse would keep it from appearing to be in any way out of the ordinary or a rushed decision.

Justin was amused at how easily and pastorally the Bishop was as he spoke about their being able to be together in that arrangement. There appeared be no need for attempts at disclosure or explanations about the nature of the situation, as the facts were blatantly obvious to both of them, Justin thought to himself how thorough, and capable Marc had been at handling the question. He was also warmed and impressed by the Bishop's attitude and understanding, especially as the issue seemed currently in the Church to be such an elephant in the room for many, even though most clergy and laity were quite aware of the elephant.

During the train commute back to the Abbey Justin's thoughts continued to explore and analyze the interview with Bishop Halpin. He pondered about the unfortunate way in which the issues of attraction and abuse had somehow become so intertwined and began to recognize that he himself harboured some quite strong feelings of anger against both the press, which so often feeds upon issues of sexuality, and against Christians who often behave in the same way the press does. To reduce such complex issues to black and white simplicity, he thought, is certainly contrary to the tenets of the gospel. He mused how astonishing it was that in the 21st Century this mindless, simplistic approach seemed to be about the only characteristic that spanned the whole spectrum of Christian diversity, from the most peculiar of protestant sects to the Catholic Church.

NINETEEN

The Michaelmas Term was now just around the corner and before long the first groups of seminarians would soon begin to arrive. The first to arrive will be the new first year group who will spend several days on retreat and then two days of orientation. With yet another flurry of activity beginning, the fact that Marc would not be among the students this year finally hit Justin. He would miss his presence dreadfully this time, as they had grown so close to each other, although, as before during the summer months Marc was a thoroughly devoted correspondent. In a recent letter he had suggested that perhaps they could arrange to spend a few days at Ashley Hall, perhaps in the week after Christmas and before the New Year began. He would talk to his Pastor and see what might be arranged. For Justin, that would undoubtedly work out well, but he also would do a preparatory enquiry with Father Kevin.

Thoughts about Marc's house had frequently occupied Justin's thoughts, especially now that this idea about living there had been conceived. He thought it interesting that Marc had never really talked about it very much and he had no idea of the actual location or size of the place, except that it was somewhere between London and Oxford.

✠

Orientation and the routine of the Seminary began without incident. There was quite a sizable group of new students this year and Justin became engrossed in leading them into the mysteries of theological studies as they touched upon the sacred scriptures. In one sense he found it difficult to believe that this was the beginning of his fourth year at the Abbey. His work was extremely important to him and he applied himself to it with zest. The letters from Marc were quite frequent and they made the distance between them much easier to bear—and in any case the Christmas break would soon be upon them.

Father Kevin dropped by Justin's rooms one evening after dinner to check on how things were going. He asked about how the new first year students were managing with his courses and Justin was able to give an update on any issues. For the most part, things were working well and Kevin was happy to hear that news. In the conversation he asked Justin about how Marc was doing at St. Benedict's. By this time Kevin had met with Bishop Halpin and knew of the master plan that had been put into place, in fact, in all likelihood Kevin had been a part of its design. Justin thought that Kevin must have been somewhere in the background of all the planning that had transpired and knew that he was happy for them.

TWENTY

Michaelmas Term seemed to fly past unusually quickly. Several of the new seminarians were finding a certain amount of stress in dealing with Justin's introduction to the New Testament. It was in most cases principally their realization of the complexity of the historical documents and the historical critical approach to the texts and their origins. Justin spent an exceptional amount of time outside of classes dealing with these young men in individual sessions, which kept him quite busy. He knew that this would happen, as it had with previous first year students, and he was also confident that once they got over the initial shock they would begin to settle down with a more realistic understanding of the subject. He smiled to himself as he thought about the problem knowing that it is mostly the result of parish upbringing in which a priest must present the gospel in spiritual terms, which often gives the impression that the words of scripture are simple and straightforward. He realized from his own experience that no priest wants to, nor is expected to preach doubt. And so it is that the great crisis of faith for some often occurs right at the beginning of seminary training.

The colours of fall gradually dissolved to browns and blacks as winter set in, in spite of the fact that the English winter was not usually very harsh, but rather tended to be rainier. December brought with it the new beginning of the Church year—Advent— and with it the unpleasant recollection of Nigel's death. Justin had loved the season of Advent until that dreadful situation which had now rather tarnished his sense of joy and expectation, although life had now taken a pleasant turn. He knew that it was now time to let go of the past and press on with a renewed sense of life for the future.

Marc had written some time ago about the possibility of their taking a few days after Christmas and going to stay at Ashley Hall for a brief holiday. He had written again recently mapping out the exact dates that might be possible to see if Justin would be free to visit then. All seemed fine for those times when Justin had talked about it with Father Kevin— after all, it would fall within the Christmas break. The time was drawing ever closer and Justin was beginning to be excited about the thought of being with Marc for part of the holiday season. Marc's priest had apparently even offered Marc the use of one of the parish vehicles for this get-away in the country. Justin was quite overjoyed at the way everyone seemed to be assisting them. Marc's letters were always upbeat and positive, which was typical of his approach to life.

There would only be a week and a half of classes now as Christmas drew near—time to allow for examinations and to deal with end-of-term papers. Justin noticed that the students who had initially experienced some difficulty with the introduction to biblical texts were beginning to relax a little as they became more involved in actually dealing with the process of untangling them and learning more about the art of passing literature from one generation to the next.

✠

The final week of Advent came and the seminarians were beginning to leave, in many cases to be with their families or friends for the Christmas break. Christmas came and Justin thoroughly enjoyed the liturgical celebrations with the Community in the Abbey Church.

On Boxing Day Justin took the train into London and found his way to St. Benedict's Church as they had planned to leave that afternoon for Ashley Hall. He arrived just as Mass was beginning. Justin entered the church just moments before the liturgy began and was pleasantly surprised to discover that Marc was celebrating the Mass. This was the first time he had actually seen Marc functioning at the altar. Marc noticed Justin kneeling at the back and was secretly thrilled.

After Mass Marc took him into the Presbytery and introduced him to the Rector only to discover that they knew one another. It was now almost lunchtime, the Rector poured some sherry in honour of the Season, and they sat by a crackling fire in the lounge and caught up on news for half an hour before going into the refectory for luncheon. It was nice to be back in London and especially to see Marc again.

✠

The M40 was quite busy as they passed through the London suburbs and began their short journey to Ashley Hall. Justin had been asked by Marc to bring some nice, warm clothing for this occasion, although he didn't really understand why. It would be wonderful to be together for a few days and Justin was in a state of euphoria as they drove and talked. They left the motorway at a certain junction, took a secondary road heading westward, and finally entered another less travelled country road. Finally, as they came over a rise Marc pointed off into the distance and said, "You see that house in the grove of trees just there—that's Ashley Hall."

Driving on they eventually turned into a rather long driveway leading up through a grove of trees and then the full splendour of the house came into view. It was a lovely and elaborate Victorian building—buildings rather, as there was also a cluster of several cottages and a larger building that was perhaps a stable.

Marc stopped the car in front of the main entranceway and within seconds a man in morning coat appeared and opened the car door as he said, "Good afternoon, M'Lord. Right on schedule I see."

Stepping out Marc shook his hand and said, "Yes, Rodney, we made good time today. Rodney, this is Father Martin from the Abbey—my friend and former teacher."

"Good afternoon, Father, and welcome to Ashley Hall. I'll be parking the car and bringing in the bags, M'Lord, so just go on in and I'll see you presently."

As they walked toward the entranceway Justin whispered wryly, "Marc, you said you had a little house in the country."

"I didn't say *little*, I think I just said *house*."

"And My Lord!" Justin said in astonishment! "What is all that!"

"Well, my Dear, I know I didn't really go into detail about all that, did I. I suppose I thought it would be best left until later. But the truth of it is I inherited the house along with Father's peerage. So, although it is purely accidental, I one day discovered that I was the Viscount Sinclair of Ashley."

"Well, Marc, this is all quite fascinating."

"There is a humorous side to all of this, you

know, which will amuse you. I believe I told you that the Bishop and I have been, well, rather good friends for some time. When he discovered all of this he found it quite comical and began calling me *'My Lord'*. Of course I often used the same form of address for him—and well, we both found it rather fun—sort of a private joke. *'Yes, M'Lord—no M'Lord.'* He has quite a sense of humour you know."

"Well, I have the feeling that you know him a little more intimately than I do Marc."

Entering the foyer they were met by a matronly woman who seemed to come from a door down the main hallway.

"Good afternoon, M'Lord," she said with a cheery smile.

"Nice to see you again, Marie. It has been awhile hasn't it! Oh, Marie, this is Father Martin our houseguest for the next few days. Father, this is Mrs. Stone."

"Happy to meet you Father—we have heard quite a lot about you. I hope your stay is pleasant."

Marie continued, "Rodney will be bringing luggage and bags in and taking them up to your rooms shortly."

"Thank you Marie. We'll go on ahead. Oh, dinner at the usual time, I presume!"

"Yes, M'Lord."

"Come Father, and I'll show you to your room," Marc announced, and they headed for the grand, semi-circular staircase. Reaching the first floor,

Marc led the way along a corridor and opened a door on the right. "This will be your room Justin. Mine is the next room and it is also accessible through that adjoining door," he said with a saucy wink, indicating a door to the left, which he proceeded to open. Both rooms were similar in size but decorated differently and very tastefully.

"Let me take you on a little tour of the house," Marc suggested, "Then we will have ample time to rest a bit and prepare for dinner at 8 p.m. Of course we'll have cocktails before dinner. Let's begin upstairs."

They took another staircase up to the top level where there was a salon and a quite beautiful solarium where some exotic, tropical plants flourished. It was temperature controlled and quite humid. Then down again to the second level where their rooms were situated, which also had a lounge with a huge fireplace, then finally to the foyer level where they had entered. Justin noted as they toured that there seemed to be perhaps seven or eight staff, which would certainly be needed to manage such a house. On the main level at the back of the building was a sizable chapel and Marc mentioned that they could use it for their offices and Mass each day.

Then, a brief look at the grounds. There was a rose garden, which of course, was in its winter mode with many of the plants covered in protective cocoons against possible frosts.

As they approached the larger building at the

back of the house Marc said, "You probably noticed this building as we drove up. It's the stable. We have some horses, that was why I asked if you could pack some heavy, warm clothes. I was assuming that, if you want to, we could ride a little."

"You know, Marc, I've never ridden a horse before and wouldn't want to disgrace myself."

"Don't worry, we have a very gentle mare and she will be perfect for you. I can give you a few hints about riding and Nellie will just follow after me. Let's go in now and I can introduce you."

Entering the stable they encountered a groom who was working just inside the main entrance way. "Oh, hello Frederick," Marc said warmly, "So good to see you again."

"Thank you, M'Lord, and likewise I'm sure. We've been looking forward to your visit."

"Frederick, this is Father Martin—Father, this is our stable manager, Frederick Sloan."

"Hello Father, nice to meet you."

Marc explained to Frederick that he was taking Father on a little tour of the place and to introduce him to Nellie, explaining that they might take a ride during the next few days. Marc led the way to the stalls and they soon found Nellie and introduced her to Justin. She was mottled brown and Justin thought to himself that she had the most beautiful, trusting eyes. Justin thought that this must surely be his first time ever in a stable and he was intrigued with the smells and the sounds of snorting and whinnying.

He followed Marc's lead in tousling Nellie's mane but was a little nervous about offering her some oats as Marc did on his hand. Marc assured him that she wouldn't bite him, but that he should take care to hold his palm flat, and that the worse that might happen would be perhaps a little saliva on his hand. He reassured Justin that there was a water trough and some paper towelling where he could deal with that.

"Before we leave the stable Justin I want to show you my favourite. He's here in this stall and his name is Rider. As you can see, he's a black stallion. He can sometimes be a little frisky, but I rather like that. But don't you worry about Nellie—she knows exactly what to do and will be no trouble."

They left the stable and wandered behind it where there were lovely open fields. It appeared that the estate must be quite large, although Justin didn't feel comfortable asking too many questions about that—he was simply overwhelmed.

Eventually, they wandered back to the house as darkness was beginning to encroach upon the afternoon. There would be plenty of time to rest a bit before preparing for dinner. Marc had told him earlier that Marie was arranging to prepare his favourite lamb dish, especially as he knew that Justin was also fond of lamb.

✠

After a little rest and freshening up it was time for drinks and then dinner. A knock at Justin's inside door brought him back to reality and before he knew it the door opened and Marc was peering in with a broad smile on his face. "Are you ready to go down for a drink now?"

"Yes, I'm almost prepared Marc. I'll just put on my shoes and we can go."

"This is so pleasant, my Dear, having you all to myself."

"Well, we're not quite alone you know."

"Don't worry about that. We'll have a pleasant drink and dinner and then later when everyone's settled down in their quarters we'll be quite alone. Let's go down to the salon and have a drink."

"All right, I'm just about ready. You know this is all very comfortable Marc."

"Yes, I'm feeling rather comforted being back at home."

Entering the salon they discovered that one of the staff, Edward, was expecting them and prepared to pour cocktails. Justin chose to have a neat scotch and Marc a whiskey sour. Justin was duly impressed with the surroundings and the staff with their courteous demeanour and starched and tidy livery. They took seats near the fireplace and in a moment or two the drinks were set down. Marc introduced

Edward who was a long time member of the staff—he was a mature, distinguished man with a pleasant attitude. Marc proposed a toast to the commencement of their holiday and lifted his glass to Her Majesty. Marc explained to Justin that almost all of the staff had known him from his childhood—rather like family.

Savouring their drinks and watching the glowing embers on the hearth, they sat momentarily transfixed—both of them silently musing on how very peaceful and right everything felt.

Occasionally Edward appeared to see if he might refresh the drinks. Justin was still in a semi state of bewilderment regarding this lovely house as well as Marc's sweet smile and gracious attitude. Marc, watching Justin staring at the fire, was having almost exactly the same thought. Their eyes met finally and they smiled broadly and instinctively in one coordinated motion silently raised their glasses, then began to chuckle. Words seemed to be entirely passé.

At about ten minutes to eight, Edward appeared again to ask if they wished another refreshment of the drinks before dinner and to announce that dinner would be served at eight. They decided to have only a small splash. Justin thought to himself how utterly lucky he was and how wonderful it would be living in this house with Marc. He realized why Marc had been reticent to tell him too much about Ashley Hall and his actual situation. He surely was a young man very wise for his years.

Marc took Justin's empty glass and placed the two of them on the drinks trolley after which he rejoined Justin at the hearth and they stood for a few minutes luxuriating in the warmth. Momentarily, Edward appeared again and announced that dinner would be served in a few minutes and that they might be seated. Marc motioned to the table and guided Justin to his place then took his accustomed place at the head of the table. Marc offered a benediction and they sat. Edward came in from the kitchen again and poured a nice Riesling. Within the blink of an eye, two other servers arrived, each bearing a fish soup starter. Following, in due course came the lamb curry, which Marie had promised. To compliment it Marc had chosen a nice bottle of claret, which was soon decanted by Edward. With so much attention from the staff their conversation was a little restricted, but they chatted about the countryside and the possibility of going for a ride the next day. Justin expressed a little concern because of his lack of experience—in fact that he had no experience at all. Marc assured him that there would not be a problem—that the horses would simply do what they always do without any direction. He would however, give Justin a few basic instructions before they set off.

The meal was extremely pleasant and Justin noticed how careful the staff were to leave them to talk, entering the dining room only when required.

"You know, Justin, I perhaps didn't mention it before but Edward and Marie are married and they have been here since I was a little boy. They are very kind and I believe they, or should that be *we* think of each other as family. They are also catholic, and of course they were overjoyed when I converted."

"Interesting, they certainly do seem a pleasant couple, and they're obviously devoted to you."

"I think I should talk with them tonight and make a definite time for mass tomorrow morning. I'm sure they will want to be there. They've never actually seen me say mass. They came to the Abbey for my ordination though, but in the fray afterward I didn't have the opportunity to introduce them to you. Perhaps I'll suggest mass at eight o'clock tomorrow morning. We're both early risers and they are too. Then we can have a leisurely breakfast afterward."

"That sounds wonderful Marc. Perhaps I could serve the mass for you?"

"Of course, that would be wonderful."

TWENTY-ONE

After dinner Marc and Justin sat in the drawing room near the fire, sipped cognac and talked for several hours about how things might be after the year of curacy and Justin's teaching was completed. It seemed like a vague dream until now but was definitely beginning to take on a more meaningful shape. It would be a rather wonderful life it seemed —like neither of them had ever imagined.

As it drew near to midnight, Marc suggested that they might begin thinking about retiring to their rooms. Turning out lights as they went, the two made their way up the elegant staircase to their rooms.

"Justin, come in for a moment," Marc whispered. Once inside Marc pulled Justin near and kissed him. Justin responded enthusiastically. "After you get settled, do come and join me, my Dear."

"Aren't you concerned about what the staff will think?"

"No, not really. Edward and Marie live in one of those cottages you saw as we drove up, and the other staff members have quarters at the back downstairs. Everyone will have retired by now, and no one will be lurking around, either tonight or in the morning."

"Alright, if you're sure."

✠

Marc had undressed, done his night time routine and gotten into bed. He left the night table light on and after ten or so minutes heard the door to the adjoining room quietly open. Justin appeared to have turned out the lights in his room, which gave Marc a pleasant assurance and inwardly a silent giggle. He was very excited. This would be the first time that they had ever been completely alone together with such privacy.

Justin stood for a moment looking at Marc and then carefully closed the door and approached the bed. He took off the robe, placed it on a chair and leaned over and kissed Marc tenderly then lifted the bedclothes to climb in. As he did so he took pleasure in seeing Marc's naked body and when the full impact of that hit him he let out a little gasp, "My Dear, what is that!" parroting a remark that Marc had once used on him. He pulled the blankets over them and held Marc gently but tightly and they kissed passionately.

Marc leaned over to the nightstand, turned off

the lamp and they held each other and kissed again. "I've longed for this moment and even dreamed about it," Marc whispered.

"And so have I, my Sweet—I adore you."

TWENTY-TWO

They rose quite early after a pleasant sleep in one another's arms and Justin returned to his room to shave, wash up a get dressed. Just before going down to the chapel, as he was leaving his room he noticed the nicely made bed and went back to pull the coverlets back and mess it up a little to make the room appear lived in.

Marc was in the chapel when Justin arrived. They had agreed to be there at 7:30 in order to say their morning office before mass. When mass began, Marc was a little surprised that several of the other servants had come as well. Most of them had also known Marc for years and Marie must have informed them about the mass. Aside from Edward and Marie all the others were Anglican and Marc was touched that they would want to be present. At the time of communion, to Marc's surprise the whole group came to the altar rail and he was very touched —he gave them communion, except for one who

reverently kept her head bowed and Marc gave her
his blessing.

☩

Giving themselves a little rest time after lunch, they went to the stables at about two o'clock when Marc had arranged for the horses to be saddled and fitted up. Justin was still a little unsure of how he would be able to manage all of this, but he trusted Marc so thoroughly that he didn't let it bother him too much.

As they entered the stable, Frederick was almost finished the saddling and they chatted with him for a few minutes.

Turning to Justin, Marc said, "Now, up on the mounting block. To mount from Nellie's left side, you know that you must put your left foot in the stirrup; otherwise you'll end up sitting backward. Just joking! I know you realize that. So let's give it a try. Get a hold of Nellie's mane—also with your left hand, place your left foot in the stirrup and just swing your right leg up and over. Quite simple. The reins are looped over her neck—and I'm sure you will probably not need to use them very much. Gently pull on the right side to turn to the right and the left to turn to the left, and both of them pulled at the same time to slow down or stop. It all makes perfectly good sense, and Nellie will be gentle with you. When we eventually turn back to come home Rider will do his usual thing and get into a little gallop. Nellie will simply follow Rider. They love doing that, I suppose for the exercise. Just hang on, but perhaps when that happens it will be best to put your weight on your feet in the stirrups otherwise your behind will get a bit of a pounding." As Marc made that last remark he gave Justin a glance with mischief in his eye which he trusted Frederick would not notice.

The winter air was nippy as they rode out of the stable and even at 2:45 p.m. the sunlight was growing dimmer. Justin thought to himself how well things seemed to be going so far. Rider and Nellie appeared to be excited and eager for the ride as they trotted side by side. Marc had certainly been right—there didn't seem to be much direction needed for Nellie as she simply followed alongside. They had undoubtedly been on the particular circuit that Marc was planning to make.

"Will we be going off your property during this ride? I was just trying to imagine the lay of the land."

"Oh, yes Justin, I hadn't mentioned that at all have I. Well, just to give you an idea. It comprises about a hundred and twenty acres, basically going from the road from which we first entered to the buildings, then approximately over to that small ridge you can see over there to the right, and to the left as far as that copse of trees. Some of it is just scrubland—mostly grass and small bushes—but some of it is cultivated with hay, barley and oats which we need for the horses, especially in the winter. We are going to ride toward those trees on the left and then return to the stable from there. It's one of the usual circuits that we make on rides."

"What about fox hunting, Marc! Do you ever do that?"

"Oh, you want to go on the hunt do you?" Marc said, laughing.

"No, not at all."

"Well, some people seem to enjoy it—I don't know why, but I think it is barbaric and have never become involved. I suppose it is more for the camaraderie and excitement—and I don't doubt that the flasks of whiskey are part of that, but I think it is just cruel. And I've never heard of anyone eating a fox!"

"I quite agree. I've always wondered why some people do it, and have guessed that it must be simply some kind of tradition.

"Well, yes, you are right. But I think also that there is a certain amount of showing off involved in it—you know, riding skills and horses. I think it is just silly."

Approaching the copse that Marc had pointed out an hour earlier they stopped momentarily at a brook where the horses seemed eager to drink.

"Now Justin, when we reach a certain point just beyond those trees the horses are going to want to run for home—they are so used to that routine, so be prepared. You will be all right, I'm sure. Just hang on and put your weight on your feet and you'll be fine."

Marc's words were soon proven true and off they galloped. Marc looked back occasionally at Nellie who was following to ensure that Justin was coping and he certainly appeared to be—it looked like he was having a marvellous time judging by the broad grin on his face. Marc thought that surely Justin must have ridden before, but when asked back at the stable Justin explained that he hadn't, but that the advice Marc had given had been extremely helpful and that the ride had been very refreshing.

TWENTY-THREE

These three days together at Ashley Hall were so very important to the unfolding of Justin and Marc's saga. They were able to be completely together for the first time even though it was a brief period of time and to gain a feeling for how their lives together might work over the long term. Naturally, they realized that when they were working in the various mission parishes their days would be more structured and filled. Living at Ashley Hall would certainly be a pleasure for Justin considering all the wonderful amenities and indeed, being with Marc. For Marc it would be a continuation of his life as it had been for so many years, but with the delight of being with Justin. It was simply a dream come true for both of them.

The morning of their departure from Ashley Hall was even pleasant although they were both quite aware that now they would be separated for months at a time. After mass and a leisurely breakfast their bags were brought down to the car and the staff gathered to say goodbye. It seemed to Justin to be like a family seeing their son off. The atmosphere did not at all seem like one of employees simply doing their expected work. As far as Justin knew they did not yet realize what was going to unfold in perhaps eight months' time—but Marc, in his usual diplomatic way, would reveal the plan in due course. As Justin observed Edward, Marie and the others chatting with Marc and saying their goodbyes, he mused how happy they would probably be when they discovered what the future would hold for the house. Surely, with Marc coming to live at home again there would be a renewed life at Ashley and he felt that having interacted as he had done with them, they would delight in his being a part of the family.

The drive back was pleasant although it did have a slightly sad ambience because the holiday would soon be over. Marc did his best to prolong their time together by deciding, as he had the use of the parish vehicle, to take the ring road bypassing London and driving Justin back to the Abbey. The conversation on the trip back was filled with thoughts and plans for life together at Ashley Hall. Knowing that the hiatus until that happened would be relatively short made it less of a worry and they would both be very busy in the meantime with their work. Then, there would also be other occasions when they would be able to spend a few days together.

Arriving at Basingshore in mid-afternoon, Marc said his goodbyes and decided that he would just push on back to London rather than get involved in conversations with whoever might be around in the Seminary as it would simply prolong the agony of parting and delay his drive into London, especially at that time of day. Before leaving the car Justin gave Marc's hand a squeeze, mouthed a word of goodbye, and remarked about what a splendid time they had spent together.

'It is amazing how very fast the time seems to fly by when one is busy', Justin thought to himself as he took a brief break from reading through an assortment of term essays one March evening. His thoughts of Marc were frequent and he missed him greatly, however, it was tolerable because there was a definite end in sight. The Bishop and the Abbot, together with Father Kevin had decided that sometime in July would be an appropriate time for Justin to finish his time at the Abbey and also for Marc to finish his curacy in London.

It would soon be Easter break and that would mean that Justin would be able to spend a few more days with Marc at Ashley Hall. That would be the next significant time they would be able to see each other before actually taking up residence at Ashley.

There would also be another important task

during the Easter season, which was a visit from Brother Bede who would be visiting the Abbey for a week on his Easter break from the university in Rome. They would have plenty of time together to pass on records, notes and have discussion about the New Testament courses and the Greek classes as well as discussing other issues about teaching at Basingshore. Justin was pleased to discover that Brother Bede would be returning to the Abbey in August and would have time to settle in before the Michaelmas term began.

TWENTY-FOUR

One morning just after the term had begun
Justin left the refectory after breakfast and passed
by the cork notice board in the main hallway on his
way to his first class. He stopped for a moment to
see if there were any items that he should know
about. Attached to the board with a red drawing pin
was a sealed envelope with his name on it. He
thought this was unusual because normally notes
were left there without any concern about the
contents. Opening the envelope he found that it was
from the Principal, Father Kevin. The *note* was more
like a letter explaining that a rather disturbing
communication had been received by Father Abbot
and that Justin, Kevin and Abbot Placidus must meet
later in the day. The place and time were designated
and the meeting was planned to take place within
the monastic enclosure.

The day passed ever so slowly for Justin and he
tried to concentrate on his teaching. He could not

seem to expunge the thought of this meeting from his head, continually brooding about what might be so urgent. Eventually, the last class of the day ended and soon the meeting would get underway.

Justin took his briefcase and several books back to his rooms and decided that he had enough time to slip into the seminary refectory for a cup of coffee before going to meet with Father Abbot at four o'clock. There were very few in the refectory at that time so he was able to have a quiet few moments alone after many hours of lecturing. Placing his cup on the wash-up cart, he made his way into the monastic building and found Father Abbot and the Principal waiting.

As he entered and greeted them Father Placidus motioned toward a chair and said, "Please have a seat Father". Without any further pleasantries, he reached behind him and drew from a table a large envelope and before opening it he remarked, "This is a little sensitive, I would venture to guess. It has to do with that little flare up some time ago about Teilhard de Chardin."

"Oh no!" Justin remarked with almost a moan of anguish.

The Abbot opened the package and drew out the typical Vatican style letter with its red wax seals.

"This is from the offices of the Congregation for the Doctrine of the Faith and sealed and signed by Cardinal Rattenkönigin.

Justin emitted another groan.

Abbot Placidus was quick to remark, "Please don't jump to any conclusions Father. We were all quite aware of the incident at the time it happened and also how innocently it had come about. However, things have now apparently been forced into quite another dimension and we will have to see how we should respond. As you recall, Romeo returned to the Philippines some time ago and transferred to a seminary there. I'm not quite sure how his Bishop understands what really happened, but he has certainly put some pressure on the Vatican about it. I recall with some embarrassment, as I'm sure we all did, when Romeo managed to convince a London tabloid to run his version of the situation and how it emerged under the headline, "CATHOLIC SEMINARY PROFESSOR TEACHES HERESY".

Fr. Kevin joined in, "Yes, I remember that day well. And I remember that the reporter involved made absolutely no attempt to contact us to get our understanding of the situation but was just happy to latch onto a juicy headline. Apparently, whoever the reporter was did contact Bishop Halpin who tried to explain the details about Teilhard de Chardin, but that issue is so very esoteric that he seemed to grasp nothing of it in the slightest. And it appears that the Bishop knew nothing about what actually happened because it was so trivial that no one ever drew it to his attention."

"Well," the Abbot interjected, "we have a bit of a

tricky dilemma here."

Glancing at the tome from the Discipline arm of the Congregation for the Faith he read portions of it to them to give them an idea how overblown the issue seems to have become. In looking it over he quietly uttered under his breath, "Looks like the Inquisition is still at work, doesn't it."

He continued to read excerpts from the communication, which mentioned the names of Romeo and his bishop, who apparently is Monsignor Louis Navarro, of the Diocese of Talibon. That reference did not escape anyone's notice and drew smirks from all present.

Father Placidus read out a paragraph, which indicated that they would like Father Justin to come to Rome to participate in a '*colloquium*', which technically means a conference.

Father Abbot looked up over his half glasses and said, "And we all know what that means—which is not a dialogue at all, but a group from the Curia who ask questions without any room for discussion—exactly the same as what would have happened to Hans Küng if he had gone to Rome for his colloquium. To his credit he simply never went, even though he was in Rome on one occasion and personally chatted with one of the Curia from that Congregation—but vanished back to Switzerland before they realized it."

However, rejoined the Abbot, "I think that for the reputation of the Abbey and the Seminary, it might just be important that you do go to Rome and try to explain to the Curia your view of the episode and how innocently it came about in that dinner conversation. In this missive they have outlined several dates on which the Discipline group will be meeting, and I would suspect that it will take perhaps four or five days to deal with the meeting and the travel time. The Seminary will look after your airfares back and forth, Father. I think that the matter simply needs to be put to rest once and for all."

"I think you are right Father," Justin added, "I do agree that the whole thing is just too silly for words —and I would never want the Abbey or the Seminary to have any kind of black cloud hanging over it because of such an absurd situation. Perhaps we can look over those suggested dates and make a decision about the trip. If their proposed dates don't coincide with a natural break here at the Seminary I'm sure that Father Basil would be willing to fill in for me for those few days."

"Yes," responded the Abbot, "I'm sure we can work something out. We'll look over schedules and the suggested dates during the next few days and then contact the Vatican as well as making some flight arrangements."

"Thank you Father Abbot," Justin added before they took their leave and went about their business.

TWENTY-FIVE

That evening Justin got on the telephone and reached Marc to explain the turn of events that afternoon. Marc was understandably horrified that it had come to this. He paused and thought for a few moments before continuing.

"Listen, Justin, I'm in a position at the moment to take a little time off. "If you don't object, I would very much like to join you for this visit to Rome. What do you think?"

"Well, my Dear that would be wonderful and indeed very supportive if you can manage it. I would be delighted."

"Of course, I can—and I will look after my own airfare. I have connections in Rome where I will be able to stay for the few days as well. Do you know where you will be staying?"

"I thought about that naturally and I'm sure I will be able to have a room for a few days at the Beda where I studied."

"Alright then," Marc added, "as soon as you are sure of the dates, let me know and we will probably be able to meet up in Rome."

"Thank you Marc, it will be a great encouragement for me to have you along. I'll call you again as soon as these dates have been settled. Take care, and thank you again for your support. I'll talk to you soon. Goodbye for now."

Immediately after hanging up Marc went to his books and the internet to check out the make-up of that Curia Disciplinary Commission. He had a sneaking suspicion that he might just be able to, as it were, lend a hand in this ridiculous affair—but would probably never need to reveal any of that to Justin.

He soon found what he was looking for. Just as he suspected, one of the Disciplinary Commission members was a Cardinal he had known years before when the man was the Papal Nuncio to Britain. He was Cardinal Count Mario Santoni. Marc had met him at a social event hosted by local Catholic members of the Peerage. Santoni was a member of a wealthy and influential Florentine family and had risen to his present status in the Vatican perhaps partly because of his ancestry. He was a very gracious and fatherly man who had become fond of Marc all those years ago and had spent some considerable time enjoying Marc's affable company. Marc had not seen him for years and he wondered if the Count had even realized that he had taken Holy Orders.

Marc carefully noted the telephone numbers of his offices in the Vatican, began to muse upon how he might see him, and perhaps apply a little influence with respect to Justin's dilemma. He realized that Santoni was not chairing this commission, but knew that he without a doubt wielded enormous influence over everything in which he was involved.

✠

Within two weeks Justin was able to telephone Marc to outline the arrangements that had been made with the Vatican about the colloquium and the airline and flight times to and from Rome. He then spent some time on the internet trying to make reservations on those flights but discovered that it would not be possible as they were already fully booked. As he considered that he thought that it was just as well, because if he went a few days earlier he would have more time to get together with the Cardinal and he would then be able to call Justin at the Beda when he was settled in. He would also have more latitude to work out exactly whom he would be staying with and if it came to it he could simply stay at a hotel. In any case, the flight was not a long one —perhaps a little over three hours from Gatwick to Fiumicino.

Justin called again the day after the last call.

"Hi Justin. I've just been trying to make flight

arrangements but am not having much luck. The flights you are booked on appear to be full up, but actually that doesn't matter, I suppose. Just give me the telephone number where you can be reached at the Beda and I'll call when I know you have arrived. Actually, I might just go a couple of days earlier so I can spend a little time with my friends."

"That sounds like a good idea in any case" Justin replied, "just give me a few moments to find that contact number for the guest house. I've already contacted them and a room has been reserved for me. I'm quite looking forward to being at the college and seeing some old acquaintances. Yes, here is the number—do you have a pen handy?"

"Yes, I'll jot it down."

After a brief conversation they expressed their concluding thoughts, and Marc tried to assure Justin that it would undoubtedly go smoothly and that perhaps he would even be given an opportunity to explain how the silly mess had unfolded. They then said their goodbyes and ended the call.

After hanging up Marc sat there with a dozen thoughts swirling through his head. Maybe it was better that he would have a few more days to get together with the Cardinal, in fact, instead of trying to phone him from Rome when he arrived it might be wiser to call from London well ahead and set up a dinner engagement, once he had actually booked flights. Yes, that would undoubtedly be the way to go. Then he went back to the computer and again began looking for other flights that might better fit the situation. Eventually, thanks to online booking, he was able to find a number of very reasonable flights on one of the more offbeat airlines. It seems an Easyjet flight would be from Stanstead to Ciampino rather than from Gatwick, but that made little difference whatever in the face of this emergency and it was extremely cheap—in any case Ciampino is much closer to the centre of Rome.

TWENTY-SIX

The flight to Ciampino was an early one and Marc was soon settled into a lovely *pensione* near the Piazza Navona. This gave him a chance to have a walk around familiar neighbourhoods where he had often holidayed and a chance to stop in and have a light lunch. He needed to compose his thoughts in the event he was able to get through to Cardinal Santoni later in the afternoon after the traditional *riposo*—the Italian equivalent of a siesta. It was nice to be back in Rome after several years. He was hoping that after things had been sorted out and dealt with that Justin might give him the grand tour of the Beda so he could see where his friend had spent four happy years.

✠

Returning to the hotel later in the afternoon, Marc spoke with the man at the desk to check about making a phone call from his room to the Vatican. He showed the man the number he would call and asked if there would be any additional numbers to be dialled and the man assured he that he should get through dialling it just as it was, being a local call. That was comforting. He went up to his room to further settle in and have a little rest before making the attempt to contact Cardinal Santini.

Finally the moment came when he would give it a try and he carefully noted from his jottings what he wanted to say to whomever might answer. After assuring himself that he could do it—even though speaking in Italian on a telephone was daunting because one could not see the person, or gesture—he picked up the receiver and when the dial tone sounded he dialled the numbers. The phone at the other end began to ring and soon a man's voice responded, *"Pronto. Congregazione della dottrina della fede. Posso aiutarvi?*

Marc launched in: "Buona sera signore. Sono Visconte Marc Sinclair. Sarebbe possibile da parlare con Cardinale dell' eminenza Santoni?"

"Un momento, Signore."

Marc waited for several minutes while Gregorian chant quietly wafted over the line.

The line opened up again and this time the man began with a little chuckle. *"My Lord. I detect from your accent that you are British. I am too, so perhaps we could continue in English."*

"Oh, what a relief—my Italian is rather bookish and rusty."

"By the way Sir, I am Father John, one of His Eminence's assistants. And, I am happy to tell you that I have just spoken with him in the adjoining office and he will be delighted to speak with you. Hold on a moment longer and I will transfer your call."

The Cardinal came on the line sounding as Jovial as ever. *"My Lord. It is so good to hear your voice. It has been many years, has it not, since we last saw each other in London? I am delighted to hear your voice. Where are you, if I might ask?"*

"I am in Rome, Your Eminence, staying near the Piazza Navona and will be here for just a few days. If possible, I would love to take you to dinner during which we can catch up on news and reacquaint ourselves."

"That would be a great pleasure indeed, My Lord. I'm looking at my agenda and see that I am committed to a meeting this evening—but it seems that tomorrow evening is free. Would that be a possibility for you?

"That would indeed, Your Eminence. And it will be wonderful to see you again. I have a little surprise for you—actually, two surprises—but we will get to that tomorrow evening."

"As you are near the Piazza Navona, perhaps we could go to a restaurant that I know which is just on the Piazza, called Panzirone. You will have no problem finding it. It is right on the Piazza toward the north end on the east side—opposite Sant'Agnese almost. Perhaps we could meet there at eight o'clock. I usually just wear a simple black priest's cassock when I'm out and about on unofficial business around Rome. It will be so good to see you again Marc. So, until tomorrow evening, my friend; I will look forward to it with much delight. Ciao for now, Marc."

Marc replaced the receiver on its cradle thinking how extremely lucky he had been to reach the Cardinal so swiftly and even more so that they would be able to have dinner the very next evening. Everything seemed to be falling into place as he'd hoped.

✠

The afternoon of that day was spent wandering around in the vicinity of the Piazza Navona. Marc spent the major part of the day walking across the Tiber by way of the Ponte Sant'Angelo to St. Peter's to visit the Basilica for a Mass and afterward a light lunch. He had taken a look at the menu posted outside the Panzirone in the Piazza Navona and saw that it was without a doubt a very charming place for dinner with the Cardinal, whose comments about the establishment were quite spot on.

TWENTY-SEVEN

In the early evening Marc showered and prepared himself for dinner with the Cardinal and attempted to familiarize himself with all of the salient points that he wanted to convey—especially those dealing with Justin's dilemma and the earnest hope that the members of the Curia would somehow put aside their overwhelming power and listen to reason. He dressed in a clean clerical shirt and wore his dog collar and black suit. He could not help but notice the nods of approval and reverence accorded by the people in the street as he made his way to the restaurant—a rather different attitude to what he was accustomed to in Britain. He arrived at the Panzirone at about five minutes to eight and waited outside to meet Cardinal Santone. Numbers of people were arriving at that hour for their evening meal and offered pleasant smiles and greetings to the young cleric. Punctually at eight o'clock Marc saw the figure in black cassock and broad brimmed curé cap off in the distance toward the end of the Piazza. He was too far distant to recognize, but as Marc followed his brisk steps he approached the restaurant and finally he noticed Marc waiting by the potted shrubs. A broad smile spread across his face and he extended his hand to Marc in warm greeting.

"Well, my friend, I can see what your first surprise is indeed. I had no idea that you had taken Holy Orders. How wonderful! I am delighted. You can tell me all about that once we are seated. I have taken the liberty of telephoning them to make a reservation. They know me simply as "Father" as I do come here from time to time, but I do so rather inconspicuously, as I hate to draw attention to myself and my position with the Curia. You realize, I'm sure, that priests are such a common sight here in Rome. Why don't we go in, shall we?"

Entering the restaurant they were greeted warmly by the headwaiter who showed them to their table. Soon bread and oil were brought and the waiter asked about wine. They discussed briefly what it was they were wanting for dinner and it was quickly decided that a nice bottle of Pinot Grigio would be preferable.

As the wine was being fetched, the Cardinal reminisced a little. "You know Marc, I remember well the first time we met. It was, I believe, at a reception at Buckingham Palace honouring some occasion in Her Majesty's life. They had gathered representatives of the Peerage for the occasion. I remember well how delighted I was to meet you—and then what pleasant times we were able to spend together after that time, until I was recalled to Rome. So, my friend, the Cardinal continued, tell me all about how you went from your Oxford days and where you did your preparation for Holy Orders."

"Time has flown by hasn't it, Eminence. To make the story as brief as possible, I met Bishop Halpin at a London social event in due course and we talked at some length. We got together on occasion. One thing led to another about church business and the idea of Orders eventually emerged. After finishing at Oxford I spent about a year at my country home preparing myself and contemplating the possibility. And to make a long story shorter, the Bishop encouraged me to contact the Seminary at Basingshore Abbey. I did so and eventually went for a retreat there to see what I thought."

His Eminence perked up his ears at the mention of Basingshore and said, "Oh, now that rings a bell with me for some reason."

Marc thought to himself that he was quite aware what that reason was.

Food began to be served and wine poured as they talked. They toasted the happy occasion of their re-acquaintance and expressed delight in seeing each other again. It was quite like old times when they would occasionally get together for dinner and an evening in London.

Marc continued with the thread of their talk about his studies and Basingshore. "I graduated from seminary several years ago and was ordained at the Abbey and then began working in a London parish."

The Cardinal seemed very interested and began to have the feeling that there was much more to the story which was unfolding. "Do continue, Marc, I am having a sort of *déjà vu* about all of this."

"You are quite right Eminence—you are very astute to begin connecting our meeting together and my presence in Rome at this particular time."

"I didn't realize that my innermost thoughts were quite so obvious."

Marc smiled and said, "Well, now I am going to bare my soul and confide my deepest feelings to you —and I think I know you well enough that I can do that with candour and ease. It is a rather complex story, but let me begin at the beginning."

"Please feel free, my friend. You are right about putting your trust in me. I respect, and admire that immensely."

Marc continued. "During my first year at seminary one of the monks who taught New Testament and Greek retired—somewhere in his eighties I believe. He was replaced by a priest who was not of the Community, but rather an Oblate of the Order. His name is Justin Martin. To encapsulate, over the course of several years we became close friends—and in fact fell completely in love with each other."

"Very interesting—very interesting! I'm so sorry Marc—I mean for the course things have taken. I think I have an idea what the rest of your story might be about now—however, please continue."

"Well, Your Eminence, we both realize why I am here in Rome and why I so wanted to have the opportunity to speak with you. Justin arrives in two days to attend the colloquium to which he has been summoned. I must tell you, he has no idea that I am speaking with you, or that I even know you. He thinks that I just wanted a few days away and was able to join him in Rome—to be together for a short time, as I now live and work in London and he at the Abbey teaching. Incidentally, he will be replaced by a monk who has been studying here in Rome at the end of the next term, when we will, with Bishop Halpin's blessing be living at my home, Ashley Hall, and looking after three country parishes nearby."

"Very intriguing indeed. I didn't know that the Bishop was that perceptive—and it is a good thing to hear."

Marc continued, "Now, one of the reasons why I wanted to speak with you is that I was one of the six witnesses to the incident involving a reference to Teilhard de Chardin. I know that a Filipino seminarian blew the whole incident out of proportion and tried to intimate that Justin was referring to Teilhard in his classes. Romeo—the seminarian—even approached a London tabloid about it and the headline accompanying the silly article said that a Catholic professor was teaching heresy."

The Cardinal nodded, indicating that this seemed to be part of the story he had heard—*à propos* of the letter from the Philippine bishop who was Romeo's sponsor, and the reason why this colloquium was instituted.

"The incident," Marc added, "took place after dinner one evening in the seminarian's refectory where five or six seminarians—including me and Romeo were sitting talking with Father Justin. Someone made a comment about how useful the computer and the internet were in preparing term papers and doing study related work. Justin made the remark that it was interesting that fifty years or more ago Teilhard de Chardin had spoken of a time when there would be a universal layer of communication, which he termed '*the noösphere*', would link people together in a universal sense. Romeo flew into a rather embarrassing rage right at the table and called Father Justin some indiscrete things to everyone's utter shock. Father Justin did not even teach dogmatics or church history—rather, his field is New Testament studies and Greek. It was an extremely unfortunate incident. And then the follow-up was perhaps as you have heard it. But mind you, I was only one of five or so witnesses to this event. It is true that Father Justin and others, including myself, have a profound fondness for the writing of de Chardin and there are many societies that witness to his work and deep mysticism. It is worthy of comment that Pierre Teilhard de Chardin remained under suppression until his death and maintained obedience to Rome."

"Marc, I completely agree with you and I confess to you, since you have been so candid with me, that I myself hold Teilhard in awe—but as you know, it was the Curia that dealt this blow to the poor man, and I am now a part of that system. But, as you also realize, it is virtually impossible to swim against the current on issues like this, even though I find it intellectually embarrassing and contrary to my nature."

"Your Eminence, are you yourself a Jesuit?"

"No, my Dear, there are hardly any Jesuits associated with the Curia—in fact, to be honest I believe there is some bad blood between the two, but don't quote me on that! In a strange way, perhaps that is at the core of this present dilemma. You will find this interesting. On a number of occasions during Curial Lenten retreats and quiet days, I used to carry a copy of "*The Hymn of the Universe*" with me as reading material—although, bound in brown paper covers. I'm sorry and embarrassed to say that the Curia simply did not comprehend what he was saying—and I have to admit that Teilhard's writing is extremely challenging."

"I'm so happy to hear you saying these things, Eminence, and I want to assure you that nothing you've said will go any further on my part. It is good to be able to talk so freely—and it is regrettably rather unusual."

"Marc, it is so refreshing and liberating to be able to speak to a colleague at this level—to expose the underbelly, so to speak, which I can never really do—and I want to thank you for being such a wonderful friend. I also want to offer my full blessing and good wishes to you and Justin in your lives together."

"Thank you, Your Eminence. I also appreciate your support."

Dinner ended on a very happy note and the two clerics disappeared into the shadows of the Roman night.

✠

Marc rose early on the day that Justin was arriving. He puttered with some writing after saying his office and thought fondly of Justin. He would be arriving during the early afternoon and Marc estimated how long it would take him to get to the Beda College from the airport. He would wait until later in the afternoon before trying to reach him by telephone. He might wish to have dinner at the Beda with friends, or perhaps they might meet and have some dinner together. The colloquium would take place in a few days and Justin would certainly want to have time to think about it, although there would be opportunities for them to get together for meals. He was extremely excited about seeing Justin again and was hoping and praying that the Cardinal would be able to review the case with his colleagues and indicate that he had done some preparation and that he had spoken with a witness to the incident. They would undoubtedly ask Justin for his version of what had happened.

Shortly after four o'clock Marc picked up the telephone and made a call to the Beda asking to speak with Father Martin. He was put through immediately and Justin's enthusiastic answer thrilled Marc.

"I knew it would be you Marc—and it's so nice to hear your voice."

"Good to hear you too. I've been here for two days and have caught up with a few friends and visited around the city."

"We must get together for a meal soon—perhaps tomorrow evening? I'm afraid that this evening I have been committed to dining with old friends here at the Seminary."

"Yes, I figured as much, and that will be good for you. I have no difficulty keeping busy here and tomorrow afternoon and evening would be fine. I know that your meeting with the Curia is the day after tomorrow, is it not?"

"You're right. And I do appreciate your support and especially your coming to Rome to be with me in my hour of trial."

"Don't fret overly much about it Justin—I'm sure everything will work out fine. Oh, and let me give you the telephone number here at the hotel where I'm staying in case you want to reach me. It's just off the Piazza Navona. Do you have a pen and paper handy?"

"Yes, just hold on for a moment and I'll be ready."

He then gave the hotel number to Justin and after a little more chat they terminated the call with plans to meet at a certain location the following day. Marc placed the receiver back in its cradle feeling very happy to have reached his friend and also that Justin seemed to be so up beat.

TWENTY-EIGHT

Justin and Marc met at an agreed upon time in front of a restaurant near the Tiber the next morning. Justin knew it well from his days at college and he had made a reservation for lunch. It was so good to see Justin again as it had been some months since they had been together. Talk over lunch was casual—catching up on news of their respective lives. It quite naturally gravitated toward the meeting with the Disciplinary arm of the Doctrine of the Faith Congregation. Justin filled in Marc on the discussions at the Abbey with Father Kevin and the Abbot about how the matter might be dealt with. They had all been in agreement that it would be blatantly pointless to try to avoid it—especially from the point of view of the Abbey and more especially because the whole scenario had been misrepresented and frankly so utterly ridiculous.

Marc reiterated his belief that the Curia would surely not deny Justin an opportunity to explain how he viewed what had happened on that unfortunate occasion when Romeo lost his temper and went ballistic.

Justin responded, "Well, I certainly hope you're right Marc. The whole affair does seem to be giving me some misgivings, but I suppose that we simply have to be honest and face the situation. I'm sure that the results will be just and humane."

"I'm sure they will and before we know it the whole absurd thing will have blown over."

Luncheon continued on a brighter note, the sun came out theatrically to enhance their perception on things, and they became involved in discussing their present work and the prospects of living together in the country at Ashley Hall.

✠

The following day—the day of the dreaded colloquium—got off to a good start with a nice continental breakfast in the Beda faculty refectory. Justin had risen early, showered, shaved, and dressed in his Benedictine habit. He spoke to a few sympathetic friends over breakfast and was in good humour even though he would be approaching the meeting with the dreaded Curia.

Finally, when it was about an hour before the meeting at the Vatican offices of the Doctrine of the Faith Congregation, Justin ordered a taxi, took his briefcase, and off he went to the Holy Office—and his fate. The meeting had been scheduled for the mid-morning, so he was hoping that it would end just before noon. Arriving at the Palazzo he was ushered into an anteroom to wait until he was summoned to enter and confront their Eminences.

Minutes seemed to drag into hours, but finally a minor secretary came to usher him into the grand, Baroque salon, which was set up with a table for the six cardinals and one rather lonely looking chair before it for the defendant. The council was seated and Justin was ceremoniously introduced to them by the priest who had come to summon him, although not by name—simply as the body that would examine him. He did not actually recognize any of them by name, except he thought he did find one face familiar—the Cardinal who had some years ago been the Papal Nuncio to Britain.

The Cardinal who was to chair this meeting was seated in the centre chair. He was obviously the head of this Disciplinary commission. He stood eventually, addressed Father Martin by name, and introduced himself as Cardinal Berlini, after which he invited everyone to be seated.

Cardinal Berlini began the proceedings, "Father, I am sure you are aware of the reason for this tribunal and understand why it is necessary for us to take this action. Just to place a few facts before you before we begin, you are undoubtedly aware that a seminarian from Basingshore Abbey took a complaint to his bishop in the Philippines who then contacted the Holy Office with respect to the issue, which involves information about Father Pierre Teilhard de Chardin, who you are undoubtedly aware was inhibited by this Congregation regarding the publication of his literary works many decades ago. You are aware of the nature of this present assembly, I take it Father."

"Yes, your Eminence, I am aware of the situation."

"Father, are you also aware of the newspaper article which eventually followed the incident which appeared in a London news magazine?"

"Yes, your Eminence, I am."

"And you have read, or heard, the letter which we sent to the Abbot of Basingshore outlining the reason for this colloquium?"

"Indeed, I have, Eminence."

"Before continuing with this issue, Father, I should inform you that we have spoken with another person who was a witness to the, shall we call it, conversation around which the whole issue seems to hinge."

"I did not know that, your Eminence, but I am glad to hear of it—it can only be helpful."

"We—that is, this commission gathered here before you—have deliberated over every conceivable aspect of the incident at some length based on the information we have from the Philippine bishop, a letter from the seminarian in question, from the person who witnessed the conversation as well as the newspaper article and also some contact with Bishop Halpin of London. We would like to give you, Father, an opportunity to respond to us regarding your view of what happened and why this has become such a—shall I say—lively issue."

Father Justin, raising himself from the ornate chair, in which he was seated, stood before the commission with the utmost of respect and deference. He began: "Cardinal Berlini, and Your Eminences, I am happy to have the opportunity to come before you and to offer what I am able with regard to this troubling situation."

Justin paused for a moment, as though thinking just where to begin, and finally said, "Your Eminences, when the incident occurred, I had been teaching at Basingshore Abbey for about two years. My responsibilities were in teaching New Testament scripture and Greek. I have enjoyed this work immensely and find that interaction with the seminarians has been a true blessing. Although I am an Oblate of the Benedictines I live in the seminary building in a small suite of rooms and take my meals during term in the seminary refectory, which allows me to know and share many aspects of our lives together. Out of term, I am considered to be a part of the monastic community and share in all aspects of it, including taking meals in the Community refectory, but all through the year I share in the choir offices of the Abbey, as do the Seminarians.

The Teilhard de Chardin '*incident*' happened

quite by chance one evening at dinner in the seminarian's refectory. I was sitting at a table with, I believe, about six of the students. We were having dessert and coffee or tea when the subject of computers came up. We have a computer lab in the library and one of the newer students was commenting on how convenient it was to be able to write term papers and essays on the computer and even mentioned how available information was on the web regarding just about anything one could imagine, including the news of the world. At that point I made what I thought was simply an aside about how Teilhard de Chardin had predicted some fifty years ago that the day would come when there would be a level of communication somewhat like this which he named the *noösphere*. At that moment, a Philippine first year student named Romeo Mendoza, flew into a rage and chastised me roundly saying that I should know better than to even mention someone who had been inhibited by the Catholic Church. His overreaction quite shocked me and the other students present. He finally calmed down and we thought he gained control over his indiscrete behaviour. However, it seems that did not happen and he contacted his Bishop in the Philippines as well as speaking with a London tabloid newspaper, which printed an outrageous story under the headline, CATHOLIC SEMINARY PROFESSOR TEACHES HERESY. I have a copy of the article in my briefcase if you should want to read it."

"Don't worry, Father, we have seen it. But do continue."

"Well, there are just a few more points I would like to make and I will be brief. Incidentally, Romeo left Basingshore and returned to the Philippines where I gather he is continuing his studies. In addition to that, I would just point out again that I teach New Testament and Greek where there would certainly be no reason for alluding to Pierre Teilhard de Chardin. I do confess, however, that I personally have a somewhat high regard for much of his writing —that is, what I can fathom of it, as it is quite esoteric, and I admire his obedience and silence when the Church inhibited him, but I do realize that is beside the point in this present issue. Incidentally, the reporter from the tabloid—and we have quite a few British ones which are a bit of a disgrace—never contacted anyone at the Abbey about the story. It was perhaps the usual attempt to find a juicy headline that would sell papers. To give him his due though, I am told that he did telephone Bishop Halpin about it who tried to put into perspective what the official position about de Chardin was, but the man was not really able or equipped to grasp any of it. I suspect that he just wanted to be sure that such a person even existed. I think that is really all I can tell you, Your Eminences. And again, I thank you for hearing me."

"Thank you Father Martin for coming before us and for making this journey to Rome. We will be deliberating about this and will in due course follow up on our letter to the Abbot of Basingshore Abbey about our conclusion. But, permit me to say, Father, that your account of the events of that evening match exactly with those of the other person who also witnessed that particular discussion."

"Thank you, Your Eminence."

Justin was then ushered out of the salon by the same undersecretary who had brought him in and he went on his way again by taxi back to the Beda, with thoughts of the possibility of seeing Marc for dinner that evening.

TWENTY-NINE

When Justin entered the main foyer of the Beda guest wing he found Marc sitting in one of the lounge chairs reading a magazine. Broad smiles spread on their faces as Marc stood to greet Justin.

"Well, that is over Marc and it wasn't as bad as I had imagined it might be."

"Good, I'm delighted. I made a guess at how long it might take and added in the travel time and thought I might meet you here. And I was quite close in my estimate, actually, I've only been here for half an hour."

"I'm so happy to see you. What do you think about dinner tonight? We can prowl around some of my favourite places in Rome for the rest of the afternoon and then go for a pleasant dinner and I will also be able to give you a running commentary on how the colloquium went."

"That would be very nice. I'm quite curious, as you can well imagine."

"Let's go up to my room and I can change out of this habit and then we can go out to sightsee, relax and enjoy this lovely weather."

"That sounds like a good idea. After all the pressure that has been building up in you a nice relaxing walk will be welcome I'm sure."

✠

The walk along the Tiber and through neighbourhoods that Justin knew was extremely relaxing. He pointed out numbers of restaurants and coffee bars that he had frequented as a student. Occasionally, they would stop for a bite to eat or something to drink as Justin explained exactly what had gone on that morning at the Vatican.

"After a review of the letter that was sent to the Abbey—the one that the Abbot and Father Kevin shared with me—Cardinal Berlini, who chaired the colloquium, asked a few questions about Romeo and how he was adjusting to studying in Britain. I admitted that I didn't really know him that well, but that I did realize that he had brought his rather dogmatic, right wing Catholic attitudes with him. I also remarked that I had been quite taken aback by his violent reaction to any mention of Teilhard de Chardin. It is my guess that that Romeo, in his letter to his Bishop, gave the impression that I was teaching de Chardin's ideas in the course of our class work. However, after preliminary questions and my succinct answers, Cardinal Berlini asked if I would explain my view of what happened in the refectory, which I did. And also, during the session he happened to mention that they had also spoken to another person who was present and witnessed the outburst. I thought about that a good deal afterward and came to the conclusion that they had certainly done their investigation rather thoroughly.

"In any case," Justin continued, "Cardinal Berlini at the very end of the session did make a comment that I found rather intriguing—and he needn't have told me I wouldn't have thought. He said that my recounting of the incident matched up exactly with the account of the other witness. I found that somewhat reassuring."

"I should say so," Marc countered.

"However, the meeting ended with the Cardinal telling me that they would deliberate over the matter and follow it up with their conclusion in writing to the Abbot of Basingshore, which I suppose would be the logical progression of things."

"Well, my Dear, I'm sure that all will turn out happily in the end."

They walked on in silence for a time undoubtedly mulling over in their own minds the various aspects of the encounter at the Holy Office. It was pleasant being with Marc and just wandering around the Eternal City. The following day they would each take their separate flights back to London.

As darkness fell and dinner hour approached they happened to be very near the Spanish Steps and Justin mentioned a good restaurant that he knew and suggested that they might have dinner there. They were soon upon it, and it did look cosy and welcoming so they entered and enquired about being seated. The Maître d' assured them that he had a nice quiet table for them and led the way to it. Dinner was a delight and their last evening in Rome extremely relaxing. Justin expressed his appreciation to Marc for his being there at this rather stressing time. His love for Marc gave him a wonderfully warm feeling deep inside.

THIRTY

During the summer months there was much activity as Justin prepared to hand things over to his successor and Marc cleared away or passed on work that he had been involved with for the past year, as well as preparing for the move to Ashley Hall. They had both arranged to pick up the vehicles they would be using which would be underwritten by the Diocese. This was really a gift to the parishes where they would be working, provided by the Diocese, especially as there would be no need to supply accommodation. Marc had made it very clear to Bishop Halpin that *they*, as he underlined, would be taking care of their own living expenses.

At some stage in this time of handing things over, the Abbot and Father Kevin asked Justin to come to meet with them. It was to look at the follow up letter that had recently arrived from the Congregation for the Doctrine of the Faith. Father Abbot had already read the tome but he passed it to

Justin and then to Kevin to see what the decision was concerning the colloquium. It was rather brief, but in the usual Vaticanese language it expressed the Disciplinary Commission's decision to simply drop the issue. It also stated that the event in question had simply been an innocent remark in an after dinner discussion and that it had been blown out of all proportion. The three of them had a chuckle and joked about the inconvenience and cost of making a visit to Rome to finally arrive at what was obvious from the beginning.

THIRTY-ONE

The first week of September found the move and all other complications taken care of and the process of settling in began. That was quite naturally somewhat easier for Marc to do as he had lived there for most of his life. Justin found it a tad more complex—especially with the size of the estate and living with the aid of servants.

Soon after they had experienced the first few weeks of the new parish work, they invited Bishop Halpin to dinner one evening—an informal inauguration of this new mission endeavour.

Marc was watching the drive for the approach of the Bishop's car and before long he could see it turn the corner and approach. Edward had been alerted and was also waiting near the entranceway. He was quite excited at having the Bishop visit Ashley Hall as he had met him several times before and at Marc's ordination. The car drew up at the porch and Edward scurried out to greet the Bishop.

"Good evening, M'Lord, welcome to Ashley Hall."

"Hello Edward, so good to see you again."

"If you leave the motor running, M'Lord, I'll park the car for you."

"Thank you, Edward."

Bishop Halpin approached the stairs and in a flash Marc was there to welcome him.

"Welcome to Ashley Hall, M'Lord," Marc said enthusiastically.

"Thank you, M'Lord," he returned. They both broke into laughter as they revelled in this—their private joke.

Justin appeared in the hallway, welcomed the Bishop and offered to take his coat. After a little introductory small talk they moved into the grand salon where Edward had set a crackling fire in the hearth. Edward soon reappeared pushing the drinks trolley with its tinkling bottles and glasses and offered refreshments all around. He was quite obviously excited in his demure way to have a part in the Bishop's visit.

"This is very heart-warming on a cool September evening," the Bishop commented as he surveyed the salon.

Edward asked Bishop Halpin what he would like to drink and the reply was, "Oh, Edward, I think I'll have a gin and tonic tonight."

He knew what Justin and Marc usually preferred, but dutifully asked and having that confirmed he then proceeded to the trolley to prepare refreshments. Within a minute or two he was back with a tray, they were given their drinks and Marc proposed a toast. "Cheers, M'Lord," then they sat to relax and chat awhile before dinner.

Conversation was pleasant and the Bishop heard all about how the first few weeks of parish work had progressed and asked a few questions about their thoughts. He was certainly a very pastoral man who was open to suggestion and eager to listen.

The conversation was light and convivial and it was a delight for them to sit and relax together; something they had not really done before, as there were normally crowds of people around.

Edward appeared occasionally to refresh drinks and then near eight o'clock he came in to inform them that dinner would soon be served. Marc led the way to the dining room and motioned to the Bishop the seat at the right of his seat at the head of the table and Justin stood behind the seat on the left.

"Bishop," Marc offered, "would you be kind enough to ask a blessing?"

"Of course," the Bishop responded, making the sign of the cross. "*Benedic, Domine, nos et haec tua dona, quae de tua largitate sumus sumpturi. Per Christum Dominum nostrum. Amen.*"

As they took their seats Edward was soon at the side explaining the menu then he went to the sideboard and prepared to pour some claret into their glasses.

"In a moment" M'Lord, "the starter will arrive," Edward, announced. He then departed through the swinging door to the kitchen for a few moments and soon an Italian meat soup was brought and served.

"So," the Bishop asked, "how have the first few weeks gone for both of you? Have you had a good response?"

Justin dutifully waited for Marc to respond, but he looked over and said, "Well, Father, why don't you begin?"

Slightly startled, Justin said, "Well, actually, yes there has been what I think was a very good beginning. We have worked out a Sunday routine between the three parishes in which, because there are three points in the mission, we each say mass at 9:30 at two of them and then get together for an 11:00 mass at the third. We work it so that the routine varies and so that we can have teatime after the third mass and socialize a little. I think it should work fairly well—but we will give it a bit of time to see how it works."

"Yes," Marc exclaimed. "For the 11:00 a.m. mass we are able then to share the celebrating and preaching. The two groups that meet in Anglican churches seem to be quite keen and the Anglican clergy have been most accommodating."

Justin added, "Yes and the group that meets for Mass in the community hall seems to be very grateful to have weekly contact. I think it will work very well indeed."

"That is wonderful," the Bishop responded.

The soup bowls were collected at this point and a lovely roast of beef brought out on a platter along with the vegetables and gravy. This made a brief interruption in the conversation, but before long they were back to the topic.

"I think it will work out very well," the Bishop remarked. "And I'm sure that the people in those tiny mission parishes are overjoyed. Well, I know they are because I've been in touch with some of them and they are all very happy. I'm certain that this will prove to be a most commendable arrangement."

"I think so, M'Lord," Justin added, "and as time goes by we will have a better idea of just what might develop. And let me say, Bishop, that we are so very grateful for your sensitivity and thoughtfulness concerning our situation and that you have enabled this to fall into place."

"It is good, Justin, and I believe it will work very well. Of course, you know that I've been very much aware of the anguish and difficulty that you have suffered in the past few years. I feel quite a sense of empathy and even personal responsibility."

"That is so kind of you Bishop."

Marc chimed in, "Hear, hear. Let me second that!" and raising his wine glass he proposed a toast to the Bishop and the whole situation in general.

The conversation drifted on to other things and presently a dessert was served after which they returned thanks and moved back into the salon. Edward dutifully appeared to open a new bottle of cognac and pour three glasses. The fire in the hearth was so pleasant and the cognac, a final touch to a wonderful meal. They sat and continued the conversation until it was getting quite late. Marc suggested that the Bishop might want to stay overnight, but he had to decline the offer as he had commitments in the morning at the cathedral and felt that at this late hour the motorway would not present any difficulty for the drive into London.

Before retiring for the evening Edward had brought the Bishop's car around to the main entrance and given him back his keys. Goodbyes were exchanged as they emerged into the dark and chilly night. Bishop Halpin was soon on his way back to the city.

It was nearly midnight now and Edward and the staff had retired for the night. The doors locked and lights extinguished, Justin and Marc ascended the curved staircase to their rooms. Justin paused half way up and said, "Did you hear the Bishop make a reference during dinner to the fact that he felt *personally responsible* for the events in my life during the past few years?"

"Yes, I wondered about that. I don't know what he meant though. I suppose he simply meant it in a pastoral way—which is nice to hear a bishop say."

"I suppose you're right—but it did sound just a little bit mysterious."

After preparations for the night and putting on his pyjamas, Marc knocked softly at the adjoining door and soon he heard Justin say, "Come in." He entered and was instantly in Justin's arms.

325

THE END

About the author:

Father Dodman was born in 1937 in Vancouver, British Columbia where he was raised. He attended school, university and the Anglican Theological College of B.C. in Vancouver. He studied the violin for much of his youth and enjoyed playing in various amateur symphony orchestras over the years. During teen years there was a great interest in ships and the sea. For a time he thought that he might have a career as a ship's officer and to that end he was involved with the Royal Canadian Navy as a reservist for five years.

He was ordained a Priest of the Anglican Church in 1970 and served in various parishes from B.C. to the Province of Quebec.

In retirement for the past 15 years, he lives in Vancouver with his soul-mate of 11 years and enjoys city life as well as writing and publishing. So far he has written an autobiography, two fiction novels and is working on another project, which is in the last stages of writing.

Other books by Fr. Dodman:
A Priest's Tale: Autobiography of a Gay Priest
Troubled Seas